Mendax the Mystery Cat

Kate Saunders worked as an actress until she was twenty-five and then became a writer. She has written five novels and edited a collection of short stories. As a journalist she has worked for the *Sunday Times*, the *Daily Telegraph*, the *Independent* and the *Sunday Express*, and is currently writing a weekly column in the *Express*. She can be heard regularly on BBC Radio 4, presenting *Kaleidoscope* and *Woman's Hour* and appearing on *Start the Week* and *Front Row*. She lives in London and has a six-year-old son.

The *Belfry Witches* titles are Kate's first books for children. A major BBC TV series is based on them.

Titles in The Belfry Witches series

1. A Spell of Witches
2. Mendax the Mystery Cat

Coming soon

3. Red Stocking Rescue
4. Power Hat Panic
5. Witch You Were Here

All Belfry Witches titles can be ordered at
your local bookshop or are available by post
from Book Service by Post (tel: 01624 675137).

The Belfry Witches

Mendax the Mystery Cat

Kate Saunders
Illustrated by Tony Ross

MACMILLAN
CHILDREN'S BOOKS

For Elsa and Claudia

First published 1999 by Macmillan Children's Books
a division of Macmillan Publishers Limited
25 Eccleston Place, London SW1W 9NF
Basingstoke and Oxford
www.macmillan.co.uk

Associated companies throughout the world

ISBN 0 330 37283 1

Typeset by SX Composing DTP, Rayleigh, Essex
Printed and bound in Great Britain by Mackays of Chatham plc, Kent

Contents

1. A Strange Cat   1

2. An Even Stranger Christmas   19

3. Havoc   33

4. Mendax   53

5. Absent Friends   67

6. S.L.A.W   86

7. A Good Clean Fight   105

8. A New Era   123

1

A Strange Cat

"Drat!" swore Skirty Marm.

She threw her knitting across the belfry. The needles hit one of the huge church bells with a dull "ping".

"This is impossible!" she shouted crossly. "We want to get decent Christmas presents for our pals, and all we can do is this silly knitting! What's the point of being witches if we can't use our magic?"

"We promised Mr Babbercorn we wouldn't," Old Noshie reminded her. "We swore we'd give up magic and be terribly good when we came to live with the humans. And we don't have any money, so we'll just have to give everyone our egg cosies."

She held up her boggly piece of knitting. It looked more like a hand grenade than an egg cosy, but Old Noshie was extremely proud of it

1

– she had never made anything by herself before without using one of her spells. Secretly, she was rather sorry she had to give it away, even to Mr Babbercorn.

Mr Cuthbert Babbercorn was the young curate at the church where the witches lived, and their best friend. He had been very kind to Old Noshie and Skirty Marm since the amazing day he discovered he had two genuine witches living with (and eating) the bats in his belfry.

Skirty Marm pulled a dead bat out of her sleeve now, and swallowed it with an angry gulp.

"I did so want to get something special for Mr B. – perhaps a friendly little robot to do his shopping."

She stamped her foot impatiently, raising a little cloud of dust. She was a long, skinny witch with a wrinkled grey face, beady red eyes and a clump of purple hair. Her black rags were full of holes, and her black pointed hat was patched and sagging.

Two months before – the day after Hallowe'en – the two witches had been thrown out of their home on Witch Island for singing a rude song about their queen, the evil Mrs

Abercrombie. As part of the dreadful punishment, they had also been stripped of their stockings.

I must explain what a terrible thing this is for a witch. On Witch Island, the colour of a witch's stockings shows how old she is, and how much magic she is licensed to perform. Old Noshie and Skirty Marm were one hundred and fifty years old – very young for a witch – and at the time of their banishment they had been Red-Stockings. The Red-Stockings were wild young witches, hardly out of school. Witches over two hundred years old were Green-Stockings. And the most powerful witches of all, who were more than three hundred years old, were the Purple-Stockings. Every time a witch changed the colour of her stockings, her magic increased and she was given a more advanced spellbook.

On the miserable night when Old Noshie and Skirty Marm were banished from Witch Island, they had been in a very sad state – two failed witches without stockings, spellbooks or a home. They would have been even more miserable if they had known that their broomsticks had been instructed to drop them into the sea. The two brooms were faithful creatures, however, and though the witches never knew it, they performed one last act of kindness. Instead of letting Old Noshie and Skirty Marm drown in the freezing water, they left them in the quiet English village of Tranters End.

At first, only Mr Babbercorn had known they were living in the church belfry. Now, thanks to a series of strange, magical happenings, everyone in the village knew about their local witches. Old Noshie and Skirty Marm had been made very welcome. Their friend Mrs Tucker, who ran the post office, was also Brown Owl. She had not only given each of the witches a pair faded red stockings to keep their legs warm, but she had also invited them to join her Brownie pack, and this was where they had learnt to knit.

"I don't know how those tiny Brownies find knitting so easy," Old Noshie complained. "I'll never get a badge at this rate."

She was shorter and fatter than Skirty Marm, with a round, bald head (on which she wore a blue wig to keep out the cold) and sticking-out ears. The most distinctive thing about Old Noshie was that her face was bright green (not an unusual colour for a witch) and glowed in the dark. She glanced up at her friend, and squeaked, "Skirty! Remember our promise to Mr B.!"

Skirty Marm was climbing up the side of one of the bells – she was extremely nimble for a witch in her 150s. From somewhere in the wooden rafters, she pulled a bottle of Nasty Medicine.

"Just a little sip," she said, "to cheer us up. It's ages since we touched a drop and we only promised not to get drunk again."

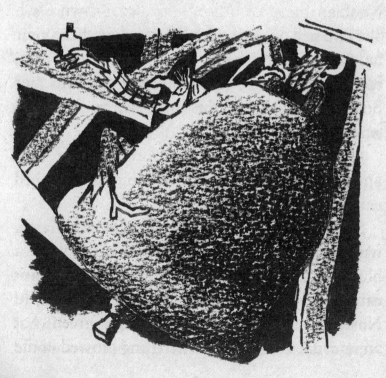

"Oh, well," said Old Noshie, "one teeny sip won't make us drunk."

Skirty Marm jumped down to the splintery wooden floor, opened the bottle, and took a swig of Nasty Medicine. As all sensible humans know, it is WICKED and DANGEROUS to drink someone else's Nasty Medicine. What is poisonous to a human, however, is often an absolute treat for a witch. Noshie and Skirty each took two large gulps.

"I feel a little better now," hiccuped Old Noshie.

"I'm still very weak and depressed," Skirty Marm said. "I'd better have some more." She took another large gulp, smacking her lips. "It's not like breaking our promise, because we actually *need* it."

Old Noshie said, "I think I could force back another drop – just for my health." She grabbed the bottle for a deep swig.

Skirty Marm grabbed it back. "You greedy old stink – save some for me!"

They struggled and fought and biffed each other's noses. In a very few minutes, the bottle of Nasty Medicine was empty. The two witches were disgracefully tipsy. Mr Babbercorn would have been horrified. But they were too tipsy to feel sorry for breaking their promise.

"Let's have a rest," said Skirty Marm, "and watch our tree."

Mr Babbercorn had found an old Christmas tree made of dusty tinsel. He had decorated it with some dented silver balls, and given it to the witches, who thought it was the most beautiful thing they had ever seen. They sat and gazed at it for hours on end, and had already decided not to take it down when Christmas was over.

Nasty Medicine always made Skirty Marm rather bold and adventurous. While she gazed at the tree, little red sparks were fizzing in her eyes – a sure sign that her busy brain was working.

"I'm not giving Mr Babbercorn and Mr Snelling stinky egg cosies!" she declared suddenly. (Mr Snelling was the vicar at Tranters End.) "They're going to have the very best – and that means presents made by magic!"

"They'll never let us," Old Noshie said, shaking her head. Nasty Medicine made her a little slower than usual.

Skirty Marm pinched her friend's ear to wake her up.

"Stupid, we're not going to tell them! We'll

give them our magic presents first and say sorry afterwards. They'll be too pleased to get cross."

"Well . . ." It was never difficult to lead Old Noshie astray. She and Skirty Marm had been best friends since they were baby Yellow-Stockings, still at Elementary Witch School. They did everything together. "What do you think we should give them?"

"Nothing too elaborate," Skirty Marm said. "We haven't got our Red-Stocking Spellbooks, after all. We don't want to do anything that's going to go wrong."

She frowned. Giving up magic had not been easy for Skirty Marm. She often wished she had thought of sneaking a spellbook out of Witch Island. At school, she had won the Spellbinders Medal for thirty-six years in a row. Living as an ordinary human sometimes seemed like a bit of a comedown.

Old Noshie, who had never won any medals, did not mind so much. She added a couple of huge stitches to her egg cosy.

"Mr B. won't be cross as long as our magic presents are useful," she said comfortably.

Skirty Marm had begun to pace up and down.

"What about shoes with wings? No – they'd only make Mr B. nervous."

The two witches poured themselves cups of warm rainwater. Old Noshie produced some salted beetles she had roasted in the vicar's oven, and they settled down to think.

"I know what Mr Snelling would like!" shouted Skirty Marm suddenly. "He's always saying his bald patch makes his head cold. Let's give him some *hair*!"

Old Noshie was impressed. "Brilliant. He'll be so pleased. But Mr B. doesn't need hair. What'll we make for him?"

"Mr Babbercorn needs an umbrella that never gets lost," Skirty Marm said. "He told me so, only this morning. He keeps leaving them behind."

Old Noshie's bright green face was anxious. "Are they difficult spells, Skirt?"

Skirty Marm liked to think she remembered most of her Red-Stocking spells – especially when she had been at the Nasty Medicine.

"Oh, they're easy-peasy," she said grandly. "Even you could manage them. The hair spell's just a rhyme and a couple of dead newts, and the umbrella will only need basic Supernatural Animation. I got one of my medals for that,

9

don't forget – when I made that automatic toad-skinner that washed itself up afterwards."

Above their heads, the big church clock chimed six. The noise made the whole tower shake. A human would have found the racket unbearable (poor Mr Babbercorn had been in bed for a week after accidentally hearing it at close range) but the witches liked a good loud racket.

"Great," said Skirty Marm. "It's time for *Cook With Enid*."

Cook With Enid was the witches' favourite television programme. They had become very keen on television while living among humans.

Old Noshie looked worried again. "Should we tell Mr B. about the Nasty Medicine?"

"No," Skirty Marm said firmly. "It would only worry the poor thing."

Feeling very considerate, they ran down the one hundred and eighty-six belfry steps to the red-brick vicarage next door. Here Mr Babbercorn lived, with Mr Snelling. When Noshie and Skirty first arrived at Tranters End, the vicar and curate had led a miserable life. An evil housekeeper, named Mrs Bagg-Meanly, had nearly starved poor, weedy Mr Babbercorn to death. Very bravely, the witches had returned to Witch Island, to steal the recipe for the magic potion that had saved his life. It had made him strong enough to drive out Mrs Bagg-Meanly and force her to get a job far away on a penguin-station in the Antarctic, but the super-strength had only been temporary. Though Mr Babbercorn's health was much better, he was still a thin, pale and generally weedy young man.

The witches found him in the kitchen, washing up the tea things.

He gave them a misty smile, through his steamed-up glasses. "Hello, witches."

Mr Snelling called from the sitting room, "Hurry up! It's starting!"

The plump vicar loved *Cook With Enid*. Every week, a smiling lady named Enid produced delicious food, which made his greedy mouth water. This week, she was showing viewers how to make a gigantic Christmas cake. Mr Snelling sat on his sofa with a witch on either side, hap-pily watching Enid's clever tricks with marzipan.

Unfortunately, just at the fascinating moment when Enid was about to spread the white icing, Mr Babbercorn put his head round the sitting-room door.

"Vicar, there's a funny noise outside."

Mr Snelling sighed. "What sort of noise?"

"That's the strangest thing," said Mr Babbercorn. "I could have sworn I heard someone shouting 'Help', but when I opened the back door, nobody was there. And now it's become the most ghastly wailing and howling . . ."

"It might be burglars," Skirty Marm said hopefully. "Shall I scare them off with a bit of magic?"

"NO!" said the vicar and the curate together.

Followed closely by the nosy witches, they went into the kitchen.

"Listen," said Mr Babbercorn, beginning to tremble.

Outside the back door, they all heard a wild, wavering cry. It curdled their blood, like the sound of fingernails on a blackboard. What terrible beast could be lurking in the dark December night?

Mr Snelling, who was rather a coward, picked up the rolling pin to defend himself. "It's a ghost . . . a murderer . . ."

Mr Babbercorn, who was doing his best to be brave, said, "Don't be silly, Vicar, there hasn't been a murder in this village for four hundred years!"

"Then we must be about due for another one!" squeaked Mr Snelling.

Mr Babbercorn nervously opened the back door. A gust of freezing air blew into the kitchen.

"AARGH!" screamed the two witches. They flew up into the air and cowered against the celling in terror.

"Good gracious!" said Mr Babbercorn.

On the doorstep, looking very small and skinny and shivery, was a little black cat. It gazed around, with big green eyes, and sneezed.

Mr Snelling had a very kind heart, even when interrupted in the middle of *Cook With Enid*. He dropped the rolling pin, bent down, and scooped the black cat into his arms.

"Why, you poor little fellow! Poor, cold, hungry little chap! Oh, Cuthbert – isn't he sweet?"

Mr Babbercorn seized each witch by a ragged shoe, and pulled them down to the floor.

"What on earth is the matter?"

Old Noshie's bright green face had paled to the colour of pea soup.

"We . . . we don't like cats," she whispered.

Mr Babbercorn sniffed suspiciously, and looked stern.

"Have you two been breaking any promises?"

"Who – *us*?" shouted Skirty Marm, very offended.

"Please don't lie, Skirty. You absolutely reek of Nasty Medicine."

Skirty Marm stamped her foot. "I'm not telling you anything until you take that nasty creature away!"

"What, this cat?" Mr Babbercorn was puzzled. "I thought witches loved cats!"

14

"Sneaky, shifty things," muttered Skirty Marm.

"Didn't you have cats on Witch Island?"

"Only the cat-slaves," Old Noshie said.

"The *what*?"

"The cat-slaves are very clever. Only the Purple-Stockings are allowed to keep them." Old Noshie shuddered. "Us young witches are scared of them. The Purples send them to spy on us. Skirt pulled a cat-slave's tail once – she had to go to prison for a week."

"I did not pull his tail!" Skirty Marm roared. "I was framed!"

"But what do they do, exactly?" asked the vicar.

"It depends what you can afford," Skirty Marm said. "The expensive cat-slaves do advanced magic and gourmet cooking. The cheap models scrub out the cauldrons and sweep the chimneys."

The little black cat mewed and nestled his head into Mr Snelling's plump neck. The vicar and the curate smiled.

"This cat won't hurt you," said Mr Babbercorn kindly. "He's obviously just an ordinary little animal, with no magic about him at all. In the world of humans, cats are simply harmless, furry pets. They're our friends."

Mr Snelling chuckled. "This one already wants to be my friend and I haven't even given him a saucer of milk!"

"Don't give it anything," warned Skirty Marm, "or you'll never get rid of it." She glared at the cat to show she wasn't scared.

"I don't want to get rid of him," Mr Snelling said tenderly. "I'm going to call him Tibbles."

In the days leading up to Christmas, while Tibbles settled cosily into the vicarage, the witches worked hard at their magic presents. Mr Babbercorn had said nothing more about the Nasty Medicine, and they both felt guilty about breaking their promise. This made them especially eager to make his Christmas gift perfect. Night after night, when the countryside was cloaked in darkness, they fluttered around the hedges and ditches on their broomsticks (the new ones they had trained in Tranters End) gathering dead newts, spiders' webs, bat spit and owls' feathers.

To their great annoyance, the cosiness of Tibbles the cat was increasing every day. Mr

Snelling fed him on chicken and cream and let him sit on his lap while he wrote his sermons. Tibbles slept in Mr Snelling's bedroom, on a tartan cat duvet. He ate out of a blue china bowl, and wore a smart red suede collar.

"It's ridiculous," said Skirty Marm scornfully. "He's totally silly about that little squirt!"

Mr Babbercorn was not quite so silly about Tibbles, but even he bought him a toy mouse and a squeaky rubber model of the Prime Minister's head. As far as the witches were concerned, Tibbles was being treated like a prince.

"I don't trust that cat," Skirty Marm said. "His eyes are too close together."

"It's not fair!" sniffed old Noshie. "Mr B. never gave *us* a squeaky Prime Minister!"

Mr Babbercorn saw that the witches were jealous of Tibbles.

"I know we make a fuss of him," he said, "but that's how decent human beings treat dumb animals. He's weak and timid, and we enjoy protecting him. But he can never be a real friend – not like you witches."

This slightly comforted Old Noshie and Skirty Marm, but it did not make them any fonder of Tibbles. He strolled about as if he owned the place. Once or twice, they even caught him in their private belfry.

"Of all the cheek!" grumbled Old Noshie. "You'd better count the mice, Skirt, to see if he's nicked any."

"Humans might like these smelly little animals," Skirty Marm said darkly, "but I'm not a human. I can't forget that on Witch Island a cat only means one thing!"

"A week in prison?" suggested Old Noshie.

"Trouble," said Skirty Marm.

2

An Even Stranger Christmas

Old Noshie sat on the belfry windowsill, watching the Eastern horizon. The moment the red rim of the sun appeared, she shouted: "Merry Christmas, Skirt! Let's open our presents!"

"Merry Christmas, Nosh," said Skirty Marm. "Deary me, it's almost a pity to take off that lovely paper. Don't tear it – we might want to frame it later."

The day before, Mr Babbercorn had placed three presents under the witches' tree – one square parcel from him, and two large squashy ones from Mr Snelling. They were wrapped in red paper with pictures of holly and robins on it. The witches had been up all night, gazing at the parcels. Both were far too excited to sleep. There was no such thing as Christmas on Witch Island, and they were fascinated by every detail.

Dancing and chuckling and pinching each other, they opened their first ever Christmas presents. Mr Snelling had given them each a cushion. Old Noshie's was green to match her face, and Skirty Marm's was purple to tone with her hair. They spent a happy half hour sitting on them, cuddling them and deciding where they looked handsomest.

"Even Mrs Abercrombie doesn't own a real, comfy cushion," Skirty Marm said, with deep satisfaction.

Old Noshie shivered. The very sound of the queen's name seemed to cast a shadow across the belfry. Mrs Abercrombie was the fattest, ugliest, wickedest old witch in the world. She would never forgive Old Noshie and Skirty Marm for singing the rude song about her – and she would certainly be dreaming of revenge for the TERRIBLE THING the friends had done to her when they returned to Witch Island to steal the potion recipe. Thanks to this TERRIBLE THING, Mrs Abercrombie's magic was no longer unbeatable and stupendous. But she was nearly a thousand years old, and horribly clever. The two exiled witches were still afraid of her.

"Never mind Mrs A.," said Old Noshie,

"Let's open our other present."

They opened Mr Babbercorn's parcel, and were so delighted that they were speechless for ten whole minutes. The curate had given his friends a fabulous transistor radio. It was neat and shiny, and far smarter than the clumsy radio sets on Witch Island.

Skirty Marm reverently switched it on. The witches sat on their cushions and listened to the news.

"Wonderful," sighed Skirty Marm. "D'you know, Nosh, I've never been happier in my life?"

"Now let's do our presents from each other," said Old Noshie. "Then we can go round to the vicarage. Oh, do hurry! I can't wait to give the vicar and Mr B. their magic things!"

They had been very careful to test the magic presents, to make sure nothing could possibly go wrong. Mr Snelling's hair-potion had been tried out on the bald head of Old Noshie, and they were sure he would love the rich chestnut curls they had chosen for him. Mr Babbercorn's talking umbrella, trained to call "Don't forget me!" if left behind, was a model of discretion and obedience.

"I think," said Skirty Marm, "we may feel quietly proud."

Their presents to each other were not surprises. They had decided to give each other their egg cosies to use as nose-warmers. Old Noshie and Skirty Marm put them on, admired their reflections in a scrap of tinfoil, and went down the one hundred and eighty-six belfry steps feeling very festive and elegant.

This was a special Christmas at the vicarage – not only the witches' first, but the first the vicar and Mr Babbercorn had spent without their

wicked housekeeper, Mrs Bagg-Meanly. Last Christmas, Mrs Bagg-Meanly (who was, unfortunately, the vicar's cousin) had cooked them a fish finger and two mouldy sprouts each. This year, the vicarage was crammed with delicious food. The witches found Mr Snelling chuckling over a newspaper called *Antarctic News*.

"Ha ha, Cousin Violet's in prison for eating penguins! Merry Christmas, witches!"

"Merry Christmas, witches," said Mr Babbercorn who was busy putting the turkey in the oven. He added politely, "What lovely nose-warmers." He had already warned Mr Snelling not to laugh.

"Thanks for our presents," beamed Old Noshie. "We just love them – don't we, Skirt?"

"They're PERFECT," said Skirty Marm. "Now, will you please open ours before church?"

"Oh, you shouldn't have," said the vicar, opening his rather untidy parcel which was wrapped in an old paper bag.

"My favourite chocolate!" He began to eat it at once.

The witches giggled and nudged each other hard. Little did Mr Snelling know that his chocolate had been laced with hair potion.

"A new umbrella! How excellent," said Mr Babbercorn. His present was wrapped in a copy of the parish magazine. "Just what I needed! You know I'm always losing them."

"You won't lose this one!" giggled Old Noshie.

"Shhhh!" hissed Skirty Marm.

They were laughing so hard, they could hardly stand up.

Two very hilarious witches followed the vicar and curate into St Tranter's Church for the Christmas morning service.

The trouble began when the village children had finished their nativity play, and the vicar climbed into the pulpit, to give his sermon.

"Dear friends," he began, "On this special morning, do you ever pause to think . . ."

Mr Babbercorn hid a yawn behind his hand. He was fond of the vicar, but nobody could call his sermons interesting. They always had to have a very loud hymn afterwards to wake everyone up. He began to worry about the lunch, and hoped the turkey was all right.

He was startled out of his worrying by a yelp

24

from the vicar. The people in the congregation were staring up at him, their mouths open in amazement.

Mr Snelling was clutching his bald head with both hands.

"Good gracious . . ." he gasped. "Good heavens . . ."

Before the astonished eyes of the village, a soft fuzz was appearing on the vicar's bald patch. As everyone watched, it thickened into glossy chestnut curls. Then it grew into long ringlets which hung down to Mr Snelling's shoulders.

Of course, Mr Babbercorn knew who was responsible. So did the villagers. Some were shocked, some were laughing, all were looking round at the two witches who were hiding their faces in their hats.

The hair would not stop growing. It snaked and spiralled past the vicar's waist. It grew past his knees, and slowly began to pile up around his feet. As the poor vicar quavered, "Help! Help!" it crept down the pulpit steps like treacle.

That terrible pair, thought Mr Babbercorn. How could they break their promise in this naughty way?

He stood up, and glared very sternly across

the church at Old Noshie and Skirty Marm.

"Ladies and gentlemen," he said, "please keep calm. It seems that our two local witches have got rather carried away with the Christmas spirit. Noshie and Skirty, remove that spell at once!"

Skirty Marm leapt to her feet. "You don't understand!" she wailed. "It wasn't meant to do that!"

She was interrupted by a sudden loud banging on the church door, which made the whole building tremble. Several people screamed.

From the other side of the door, a shrill voice – unlike any human voice – yelled, "Let me in! He's forgotten me! He'll get rained on and I'll blame myself!"

Old Noshie knocked Skirty Marm's hat off, shouting, "You smelly old fool! That's the last time I trust one of your rubbishy spells!"

Skirty Marm knocked Old Noshie's hat off and stamped on it. "I won the Spellbinder's Medal thirty-six times. This is *your* fault!"

There were louder screams, as a window at the back of the church suddenly shattered. In a shower of broken glass, something leapt into the aisle. To the gasping astonishment of everyone, including the witches, a tall green umbrella was running along the aisle on spindly metal legs. Mr Noggs, the churchwarden, began to chase the umbrella. The children clapped and laughed and yelled, "Come on, brolly! Don't let him get you!"

Once he had recovered from the first, awful shock, Mr Babbercorn rushed to help Mr Noggs. He grabbed his new umbrella firmly round the middle, just as it shouted, "You idiot! You forgot me!" and tried to put itself up.

It wriggled and struggled. One of its spokes broke free, and jabbed Mr Noggs's hand.

"Ow!" he cried. "It bit me! Let's get it into the vestry!"

Mr Babbercorn and Mr Noggs, cheered on by the whole congregation, managed to carry the fighting umbrella through the vestry door.

"Let me go!" it shrieked. "Unhand me!"

They shut it into the cupboard where the spare hymn books were kept, and locked the door securely. When they returned to the church, everyone applauded.

Mr Babbercorn wiped his brow. This was a disaster. The Christmas service was in chaos. The screams of the enchanted umbrella could be heard from the vestry. Mr Snelling, wrapped in miles and miles of hair, looked like a huge fly trapped in an enormous spider's web. His hair had grown all the way down the pulpit steps and into the front pew. Ted Blenkinsop, from Blodge Farm, was trying to beat it back with a kneeling-cushion.

The two witches were roaring at each other furiously, in a storm of biffs.

"Stupid old know-it-all! You forgot those spells!" shouted Old Noshie.

"Don't you go blaming me!" shouted Skirty Marm. "You don't even remember how to scrub out a cauldron!"

Mr Babbercorn stepped over the vicar's hair, marched down the aisle, and grabbed each witch by a bony wrist. He looked so solemn that the shouts and laughter died away at once.

"Witches, I'm ashamed of you. Remove those spells this instant!"

"Tell me the truth," Mr Babbercorn said, when they were all back in the vicarage. "Have you two been drinking Nasty Medicine again? I know I smelt it on you the other day."

"That was our last bottle," cried Skirty

Marm. Both witches were weeping. "We haven't touched a drop since! Honest!"

"Well, that's something, I suppose," sighed Mr Babbercorn. "But witches, how could you disrupt our Christmas service? I thought we'd agreed – no more magic."

"Don't be too hard on them," begged soft-hearted Mr Snelling. Now that his dreadful hair had gone, he felt sorry for the two disgraced witches. After they had removed their spells, Mr Babbercorn had sent them out of the church. Their ear-splitting howls and sobs outside the door had drowned out "O Little Town of Bethlehem" and made everyone very depressed.

"We didn't mean to!" yelled Old Noshie.

"It was meant to be a lovely surprise!" sobbed Skirty Marm. "We only wanted to get you special presents. We never dreamed those dratted spells could go so wrong!"

"It was a kind thought," said Mr Snelling, giving each witch a tissue. "After all, you do keep losing your umbrellas, Cuthbert – and I certainly need more hair." He chuckled suddenly. "Just not quite so much of it."

Mr Babbercorn had meant to be very stern, but when he remembered the look on the vicar's face as the chestnut ringlets cascaded over his shoulders, he could not help laughing. He and the vicar burst into such a fit of giggles that Tibbles jumped off Mr Snelling's lap and hid under the sofa.

"We're so sorry!" moaned Skirty Marm. "We didn't mean to ruin Christmas!"

"You haven't ruined it," Mr Babbercorn said, wiping his eyes. He was extremely fond of the two witches and didn't want to hurt their feelings. "I don't believe you meant any harm. Let's pretend it didn't happen, and have a good time. It's still Christmas Day."

Old Noshie sniffed. "We'll never touch magic again. Will we, Skirt?"

"Never!" said Skirty Marm.

"Have you ever heard of piecrust promises?" Mr Babbercorn asked.

The witches shook their heads.

"A piecrust promise is easily made, and easily broken." His voice was kind, but very serious. "No more promises like piecrusts, eh? This one should be a lot stronger."

Both witches looked even more ragged than usual. Their pointed hats were boggled out of shape from fighting and crying, and bent over like two Leaning Towers of Pisa.

"We promise!" they chorused.

Then Mr Snelling cheered them all up by producing the box of deluxe crackers Mrs Tucker had given him. Old Noshie and Skirty Marm had never seen a Christmas cracker before, and were quickly distracted from their grief – Skirty particularly liked the bangs because they seemed to annoy Tibbles. Inside the crackers were gifts, jokes and paper hats. Old Noshie got a tiny sewing-kit, and Skirty Marm was delighted with her little penknife.

After this, the rest of Christmas Day was filled with happiness. The witches and their friends ate a huge lunch. They played blow-football and watched the Queen's Speech on television. Both witches were intrigued to find the human queen so much better-looking than Mrs Abercrombie.

"She talks better, too," said Old Noshie. "She didn't even scream once!"

That evening, the witches returned to their belfry contented, exhausted, and full of mince pies.

"Very tasty," said Old Noshie. "Those humans have some good ideas about food."

Skirty Marm was sitting thoughtfully on her new cushion.

"Nosh," she said, "I still don't understand how those spells went so wrong. We were so careful to test them and to make sure we had the recipe right."

Old Noshie yawned loudly, and arranged her sewing-kit and paper crown where she could see them from her bed on the floor.

"Maybe we used the wrong sort of newts," she said.

Skirty Marm shook her head stubbornly. "Those spells were easy stuff, and I know I got them right. Any little Yellow-Stocking could have done them without looking in the book." She frowned. "Do you think our magic could be wearing out?"

3

Havoc

Boxing Day began quietly in Tranters End. Mr Babbercorn took the early service, and the only other people in church were a deaf old lady named Miss Venables, and Mr Noggs.

Mr Noggs had a plaster on his hand where the enchanted umbrella had stabbed him the day before. He was a cross, stuffy sort of man, and he looked very stern.

After the service, when the curate had shouted "GOOD MORNING" to Miss Venables, Mr Noggs said, "I'd like a word with you, Mr Babbercorn."

"Of course, Mr Noggs."

"Nobody likes a joke more than I do," said Mr Noggs, "but jokes do not belong at divine service. It's not seemly, Mr Babbercorn. I hope we're not going to see any more funny business from those witches of yours."

"The witches have given me their solemn word," Mr Babbercorn assured him. "They swear they've given up magic for ever, and I believe them. This time they've turned over a new leaf. We won't see any more strange sights."

Unfortunately, it was at this exact moment that Mr Babbercorn saw a very strange sight indeed. A pair of long underpants (pale blue, with a double cuff) was dancing up the deserted village street.

It was the sort of sight that would make most people faint with shock and amazement. Most people, however, do not have Mr Babbercorn's

experience of magic. All he felt was a terrible dismay.

"I don't believe it!" he said to himself. "The witches have broken their promise!" And he had been so sure their repentance had been real. He tried to think of some other reason for a pair of dancing pants – but what other reason could there be?

With a heavy heart, he watched as Mr Noggs turned round and saw the pants skipping along the top of the churchyard wall.

"What's going on?" he spluttered furiously. "Those are mine! Those are my warm thermals for market day!" Besides being a churchwarden, Mr Noggs was the village butcher. "You come back here!" he shouted at his thermals.

The pants danced insolently towards him – then jumped away again and whisked round the bend in the lane.

Mr Noggs turned angrily to Mr Babbercorn. "This is just the sort of thing I mean," he said. "Your witch-pals have used their spells to damage my property!"

"Let's not be hasty!" begged Mr Babbercorn. "I'm sure there's a perfectly reasonable explanation—"

"Like what?" shouted Mr Noggs. "Have any more witches moved into the village since yesterday?"

"Help!" shrieked a voice. It belonged to Mrs Noggs, wife of the churchwarden and butcher.

"Vera!" gasped Mr Noggs. "Whatever are you doing?"

Mrs Noggs was clasped in the arms of a large striped shirt. It was bouncing her along the street so violently that her grey curls jiggled.

"Help!" she shrieked again as the shirt bounced her saucily past the church.

Mr Noggs and Mr Babbercorn raced after it. The striped shirt seemed to know it was being chased. First, it bounced faster. Then, it suddenly dropped Mrs Noggs in a breathless heap, and darted away. It stood on a fence, flapping gently in the breeze, and Mr Babbercorn could have sworn it was laughing at them. He could not understand why Old Noshie and Skirty Marm had returned to their old, witchy ways. This was as bad as their very first days in the village.

"I'm afraid it looks simply awful," he said to himself sadly. "Not only piecrust promises, but crocodile tears as well. Oh, witches, how could you do this to me?"

Mrs Noggs, dusting herself down, was telling her husband what had happened.

"They all jumped out of the dryer – vests, pants, two new pillowcases, all my best tea towels – they ran round the kitchen, pulling everything off the shelves, making a horrible mess. Then one of the tea towels got the back door open! Out ran all my washing – and that striped shirt of yours made a grab for me."

She and Mr Noggs glared accusingly at Mr Babbercorn.

"I suppose those witches think it's funny," said Mrs Noggs crossly, "when decent people have to chase their own underwear."

What could Mr Babbercorn say? This was, indeed, exactly the sort of thing his witches found funny. If it hadn't been happening to a very angry churchwarden, the curate would have found it rather funny himself. As it was, he felt like crying with worry.

"I'll come home with you," he said, "and take a look at the damage. Perhaps it was a spell that went wrong – or an old, leftover spell that went bad."

Mr and Mrs Noggs lived above their butcher's

shop in the little high street of Tranters End. Mr Babbercorn turned pale when he saw the angry crowd gathered outside the shop. The moment they saw the witches' best friend, everyone started shouting at once.

The Noggs's washing had been running amok. Mrs Tucker had a pillowcase hiding up her chimney. Her next door neighbour had been locked in her own shed by two tea towels, and poor Miss Venables had been knocked down by a gang of socks.

"It's a DISGRACE!" thundered Mrs Noggs.

Mr Babbercorn hung his head. Things were looking very bad indeed.

"We welcomed those witches to this village," Mrs Tucker said indignantly, "and this is how they repay us! To think of all the trouble I took teaching those two old barnacles how to knit! Well, I'm not having characters like that in my Brownie pack!"

"First they cause mayhem at the Christmas service," Mr Noggs chimed in, "and now we're all being terrorized by my washing. It won't do, Mr Babbercorn!"

Several voices shouted, "Hear! Hear!"

"We don't mind having witches here, as long

as they can live with us peacefully," Mr Noggs went on. "But we won't put up with mischief like this!"

"I can only say," Mr Babbercorn murmured apologetically, "that I am amazed and horrified, and I'll make sure everything is put right at once—"

"You'd better!" said Mr Noggs. "Because if you're too soft on those witches of yours, I'LL HAVE THE LAW ON THEM!"

Mr Babbercorn plodded back to the vicarage with a heart as heavy as a tombstone. He dreaded facing the witches, and he dreaded telling kind Mr Snelling that they seemed to have returned to a witchy life of crime.

The vicar was in the kitchen, slicing cold turkey for Tibbles. The little black cat sat on his shoulder, his eyes unblinking circles of bright green, as Mr Babbercorn poured out what had happened.

"Impossible!" cried Mr Snelling. "I refuse to believe it! There must be some mistake!"

"I'm afraid we have to face it," Mr Babbercorn said. He blew his nose. "They've let us down."

Mr Snelling collapsed heavily into a chair.

"We must all remember," he said in a shaky voice, "that Skirty and Noshie are only very young witches. We must make allowances. We must be forgiving."

"Of course I forgive them," Mr Babbercorn said. "But everyone in the village is furious. If we just forgive the witches straight away, they'll be more furious than ever. What on earth are we going to do?"

There was a knock at the back door. Mr Babbercorn opened it to find PC Bloater, the village policeman, on the step. His normally smiling face was cold and stern.

"Sorry to bother you, Mr Babbercorn" – he did not look very sorry – "but I'd like you to come down to Blodge Farm. There's been an – an *incident* which you might be able to explain."

"What sort of incident?" asked Mr Snelling.

Mr Babbercorn did not need to ask. He could guess.

"All right, Officer," he said with a feeble smile, "I'll come quietly."

Tibbles let out a sharp mew, leapt off the vicar's shoulder, and streaked away in the direction of the garden shed.

"I'll come too," said the vicar, grabbing his scarf.

PC Bloater usually travelled on a bicycle. Today he had a police car, sent from the nearest town. The vicar and the curate got in, trying not to feel like criminals. On the way to Blodge Farm, they could not help hearing the messages that were coming in over the car radio.

It added up to a terrible list of mischievous magic. Most of the Noggs's washing had been rounded up, but some of the socks had escaped and were still at large. Three vests had barricaded themselves into someone's barn. Someone else's herd of cows had shrunk to the size of mice, run into the kitchen, and hidden under the fridge. The district nurse had been turned into a goat. This was magic run mad. Mr Babbercorn and Mr Snelling began to wish they had never allowed witches into their belfry.

At Blodge Farm, they found a scene of confusion. A fire engine stood beside a huge old oak tree. The firemen had run a long ladder up into the tree. Three of them were standing on the ladder, holding a large net.

Ted Blenkinsop, who owned the farm, was out in the lane, dancing with fury. He was a round man with a red face – and when he saw Mr Babbercorn, his red face became absolutely puce.

"Tell them to take off that spell!" he shouted. "This is a disgrace!"

"Calm down, Ted," said his wife, bouncing baby Matthew on her hip. "You'll do yourself an injury."

The three older Blenkinsop children were sitting in a row on the fence, screaming with happy laughter.

"What seems to be the trouble?" asked Mr Snelling.

"THAT!" roared Ted Blenkinsop. He pointed up into the branches of the oak tree. Through the leaves, they could just see a fireman struggling with something.

"Look out!" he called. "I've lost him!"

Something very big and weighty – it appeared to be some kind of gigantic bird – was fluttering and crashing in the branches. With a tremendous snapping of wood, it broke free and soared into the sky.

"Oh, crikey," muttered the vicar, "they've done it now!"

It was a fat, muddy pig with (Mr Babbercorn turned quite faint with astonishment) a huge

pair of wings. It swooped and curvetted through the chilly air, snorting gleefully. Another winged pig burst out of the tree. The firemen hurried down the ladder.

"Look out!" yelled Ted Blenkinsop, throwing himself down on the ground.

"ARGH!" yelled the vicar and the curate as two pigs zoomed towards them. They dropped down into the mud, and just missed being knocked senseless by a ton of flying bacon.

The winged pigs hovered over the fence. They had zoomed down because the Blenkinsop children were holding out handfuls of acorns.

"Stop that, you cheeky things," said their mother.

While the pigs were chomping acorns, the firemen tried creeping up behind them with the net. The pigs squealed, and fluttered up into the air like a pair of vast, obese pigeons.

The vicar, the curate and Ted Blenkinsop were peeling themselves out of the mud. Mr Babbercorn's glasses had fallen in a cow-pat, and he had to clean them with his muddy handkerchief before he could see a thing.

"Get my pigs back!" gasped Ted Blenkinsop. "Those animals are worth a fortune!"

"They're on the dairy roof," said Mrs Blenkinsop. "And— Oh! Look what's happened now!"

Everyone gaped. Without warning, the pigs had lost their wings. They were ordinary pigs again, very alarmed to find themselves marooned on the roof of the dairy.

The firemen moved their fire engine and put the ladder up against the wall. More messages came through on the radio in the police car. The tiny cows had also returned to normal – unfortunately, in their owner's kitchen. The goat had changed back into the district nurse. The Noggs's crazed clothes had changed back into ordinary laundry. People kept finding socks and vests in very odd places for weeks afterwards.

The attack of magic was over.

"I know who did this!" Ted Blenkinsop said furiously. He turned to Mr Babbercorn. "They've upset my valuable pigs and bust the slates on my dairy. I'LL HAVE THE LAW ON YOUR WITCHES!"

Mr Babbercorn wished people would stop calling them *his* witches as if he owned them. Frankly, at this moment, he would have loved to swear he did not even know them.

"Those pigs certainly did a lot of damage while they were flying about," said PC Bloater. "*Criminal damage*, I should say."

"Oh, Officer!" protested the vicar, "You can't arrest two pigs!"

PC Bloater said, "I didn't mean the pigs."

"You can't mean . . ." Mr Babbercorn had turned as white as his collar. "You're not going to arrest the witches?"

Through all this drama, Old Noshie and Skirty Marm had been pottering quietly round the belfry. Both were tired after the excitement of their first Christmas Day. Skirty Marm sat on her new cushion, listening to Classic FM on the new radio and feeling very cultured. Old Noshie put together a light lunch of cold mice and privet-hedge salad.

"Something simple," she said, "after all that rich human grub."

After lunch, they neatly licked their plates.

"Oh, good," said Skirty Marm, "I can hear the vicar and Mr B. coming up. Put the kettle on, Nosh." The witches did not like tea, but they did enjoy warm rainwater from the gutter.

In came Mr Babbercorn and Mr Snelling, hanging their heads. They could not look the witches in the eye, and their faces were full of sorrow.

"Hello," beamed Old Noshie. "Would you like a nice cup of rainwater?"

"Oh, witches," Mr Babbercorn burst out, "I'm not angry with you – I forgive you – but I am so *dreadfully disappointed*!"

"Dreadfully!" echoed Mr Snelling in a wretched voice. "Why did you do it when everything was going so well for you?"

Old Noshie and Skirty Marm had no idea what he was talking about, but they knew something was very wrong. Skirty Marm pulled her battered pointed hat straight, and folded her arms.

"Do what?" she asked.

Mr Babbercorn groaned. "Don't add to your crimes, by pretending you don't know!"

PC Bloater – red and puffing from the one hundred and eighty-six steps – stepped into the belfry.

"Old Noshie and Skirty Marm," he said solemnly, "you are under arrest."

The witches opened their mouths but no

sound came out. They were flabbergasted. Old Noshie's blue wig shifted as her bald head furrowed all over with wrinkles. Dangerous red sparks began to fizz in Skirty Marm's eyes.

"We only drunk the Nasty Medicine because we were depressed!" she shouted. "We needed it!"

"We're not talking about the Nasty Medicine," whispered Mr Babbercorn.

PC Bloater read from his notebook. " 'You are charged with criminal damage caused by malicious casting of spells – such as giving wings to pigs, shrinking cows, and bringing items of clothing to life. You're also charged with assault upon the person of the district nurse.' "

"I say!" protested Mr Snelling. "Assault's a bit strong, isn't it?"

"While she was a goat, she ate a magazine," said PC Bloater. "She's feeling awful."

"Well, we're innocent," Skirty Marm said proudly. "We didn't cast any of those spells. We've spent the whole morning up here!"

"That's right," said Old Noshie. "We've got a halibut."

"I think," said Mr Babbercorn wearily, "you mean *alibi*. But being up here has never stopped you casting spells before. Oh, witches, how could you?"

Old Noshie's mouth began to wobble. "Why do you just assume it was us who did that magic? It's not fair!"

"You old fool," said Skirty Marm. "Who else around here does magic? No wonder they blame us. And now the vicar and Mr B. think we broke our promise."

For the witches, the worst part of this nightmare was the heartbroken face of their best friend. Mr Babbercorn had not looked so pale and sad since the worst days of Mrs Bagg-Meanly. Old Noshie noisily burst into tears.

Skirty Marm looked hard at the curate. "I can see why you don't believe us," she said, "but I wish you could. Me and Nosh would never break a promise we made to you. You're our best human – and we'll carry on liking you, whatever you think of us."

Mr Babbercorn was deeply moved. "I'll always be your friend," he said sadly.

"Me too!" sniffed the vicar.

Skirty Marm turned grandly to PC Bloater. "All right, we're ready. You can put on the nose-irons and the ear-clamps and the leg-cuffs and the itching-belts—"

"Just handcuffs," PC Bloater interrupted. "This isn't your Witch Island."

"I don't like prison!" sobbed Old Noshie. "They make you knit metal underwear for the queen!"

"Silly," Skirty Marm said. "The human queen doesn't wear metal underwear. And her prisons aren't like Mrs Abercrombie's. We'll get a nice little cell."

"Separate cells," said PC Bloater, "to stop you making any more trouble."

"But I want to stay with Skirty!" howled Old Noshie.

"Don't worry, Nosh – I won't leave you!" cried Skirty Marm. She grabbed Old Noshie's hand, and dragged her over to the window. "Brooms!" she shouted. "At the double!"

The two broomsticks lay on the floor under one of the great bells. At the sound of Skirty's voice, they leapt into the air and whizzed across to the witches.

"What do you think you're—" PC Bloater began furiously.

He was too late. To the secret joy of Mr

Babbercorn, who could not bear the idea of his friends in prison, the witches jumped on their broomsticks and dived out of the window.

"Stop crying!" ordered Skirty Marm. "Pay attention."

She steered her broomstick down to the vicarage garden, and landed in some thick laurel bushes. A sobbing Old Noshie crashed down beside her.

"What are we doing here? We should be making our getaway!"

Skirty Marm scowled. "I'm not leaving this village until I've found a way to clear our names. We can't let Mr B. think we told lies. I won't rest until I've unmasked the real culprit!"

"The police will find us!" moaned Old Noshie.

"Not here," Skirty Marm said firmly. "And if they come, we'll make ourselves invisible."

Old Noshie wiped her nose on the brim of her pointed hat and put it back on. Distantly, from the other side of the village, they heard the siren of PC Bloater's borrowed police car. A moment later, the back door of the vicarage banged, telling them that Mr Babbercorn and Mr Snelling had returned home.

Skirty Marm led the way through the bushes to the tumbledown garden shed.

She pushed open the door – and both witches let out great gasps of shock.

"Well, well, well," said Skirty Marm in a voice of simmering fury. "I knew I was right about that cat!"

In a dark corner of the shed sat Tibbles, wearing headphones and mewing into a radio set. They had caught the real culprit – not red-handed, but red-pawed.

4

Mendax

Tibbles gave a strangled "miaow!" and tried to dart past the witches through the open door.

Skirty Marm was too quick for him. She grabbed the cat by the scruff of his neck.

"Oh no, you don't!" she yelled. "You've got some explaining to do, my furry friend! Get the clothes line, Nosh – let's tie him up."

Tibbles struggled and scratched and bit with all his might, but one small cat was no match for two determined witches. In a moment, they had wound him up in the clothes line, until he could not move one of his four paws. He lay on the floor between them, wriggling and spitting.

"I knew it!" raged Skirty Marm. "Didn't I always say this cat was a shady character?"

"You did," agreed Old Noshie. "You were right all along, Skirt."

Skirty picked up the little cat-sized head-

phones Tibbles had been using, and they heard a distant, crackling voice:

"Come in, Agent 400. Are you still receiving us?"

"Oh, it's all clear now!" thundered Skirty Marm. She pointed accusingly at the squirming cat. "This is the VILLAIN who ruined our spells! This is the SCOUNDREL who did all the bad magic in the village! All that pet business was just a cover – he's a SPY!"

Old Noshie's green face was frightened. "But what's a cat-slave doing here? Who's he working for? Oh, Skirty – could it be something to do with the TERRIBLE THING we did to the queen? Is this Mrs Abercrombie's revenge?"

"First things first," said Skirty Marm. "We must show Mr B. and the vicar that we're not wicked after all." She tucked the guilty cat under one ragged arm. "Wait till they see *dear little Tibbles* in his true colours!"

"Heh, heh!" chuckled Old Noshie, cheering up. "He'll have to give back that fancy duvet now!"

The witches peeped out of the shed, to make sure nobody was watching, then scuttled across the lawn to the vicarage.

Mr Babbercorn and Mr Snelling were feeling very sad because they thought they would never see the escaped witches again. When Old Noshie and Skirty Marm burst in through the kitchen door, their faces lit up with joy.

"My dear witches!" cried Mr Babbercorn. "Thank goodness you're safe! Vicar, couldn't we hide them from the police?"

"It would be very wrong," said Mr Snelling, wiping his eyes, "but I can't bear to turn them over to PC Bloater. We'll put them in the cellar."

Skirty Marm was grinning triumphantly. "You don't have to worry about us any more.

We've found the sneaky, hairy, smelly little SPY who did all that bad magic!"

She whipped the trussed Tibbles out of her rags, and flung him down on the kitchen table.

The vicar and Mr Babbercorn were horrified. As far as they could see, the witches were cruelly hurting an innocent pet cat.

"Really, you've gone too far this time!" spluttered Mr Snelling. "How dare you tie up my Tibbles?"

Mr Babbercorn's pale face was very stern. "What is the meaning of this?"

"This is no ordinary cat!" declared Skirty Marm. "He's a cat-slave, and he's been sent here to SPY on us!"

Tibbles saw the shocked faces of the vicar and the curate. For a fraction of a second, his whiskers twitched with the suspicion of a smirk. Then he stopped wriggling, and gave a feeble, pathetic little mew.

"What nonsense!" cried Mr Snelling. "Tibbles can't even talk – unless you've put a spell on him!"

"Talk!" Old Noshie shouted at Tibbles.

Tibbles mewed again, more pathetically.

Skirty Marm bent over the table, and put her mouth against the cat's ear.

"If you don't talk," she said, "I'll change you into a MOUSE and EAT you." Anyone could see that she meant it.

To the astonishment of Mr Babbercorn and Mr Snelling, Tibbles said, "Don't eat me! There's no need to get hysterical."

His voice was something between a purr and a mew, rather high and breathy but perfectly clear. It made the vicar and the curate feel very strange, to hear it coming from their pet.

"Name and rank?" said Skirty Marm.

"Agent 400," said Tibbles. "I'm a senior officer in the W.I.S.S."

"What on earth is that?" asked Mr Babbercorn, his eyes wide with amazement.

"The Witch Island Secret Service," said Old Noshie. "This is very worrying, Skirty. When we did the TERRIBLE THING, I thought the W.I.S.S. would be closed down."

Tibbles' mouth curved in a proud smirk.

"You have underestimated our Beloved Queen," he purred. "She found an ancient spell to call back the Power Hat – and now she's thirsting for revenge!"

"I'm completely lost," complained Mr Snelling. "What terrible thing? What Power Hat?"

"Tell them, Skirty!" cried Old Noshie.

Skirty Marm was looking more seriously frightened than her friends had ever seen her. "It happened when we flew back to the island, for the potion spell," she said. "We stole the Power Hat and threw it in the sea. We thought that if she didn't have the hat, Mrs A. couldn't be Queen of Witch Island any more. We thought she'd just be an ordinary Purple-Stocking. We thought they'd have to have a proper election."

"Fools!" chortled Tibbles.

Mr Babbercorn sat down. He was bewildered. "I don't understand. What is the Power Hat?"

The witches had never told him about this.

"It's a very magic hat," Old Noshie said in a trembling voice. "It's two metres tall, and it has a candle stuck in the point that never goes out. Nobody really knows everything it can do – but it gives anyone who wears it tremendous magickness."

"If you'd taken the trouble to listen to Witch Island Radio," Tibbles said with a mewing laugh, "on that natty transistor of yours, you'd know what happened after you did that

TERRIBLE THING. Yes, there was an election – but Mrs Abercrombie won. She was still the most powerful witch on the island, and the Greens and Purples all voted for her. The Red-Stockings weren't allowed to vote for anyone."

"Typical!" thundered the ex-Red-Stocking Skirty Marm.

"When Mrs A. called back the Power Hat," Tibbles went on, "by summoning her friends the Sea Spirits, it was business as usual on Witch Island."

Old Noshie shivered. "Oh, Skirt! Now we'll never be safe from her!"

Skirty Marm tried to look brave, but she was shivering too. Mrs Abercrombie was a witch of genius, and with the Power Hat back on her hideous head, she was the most dangerous witch in the world. This was the witch who had regularly turned her personal guards into slugs when she got bored with them. And now she was thirsting for revenge!

"So she sent Tibbles to do all that dreadful magic!" said Mr Snelling. "It was very naughty of you, Tibby. How could you let poor Noshie and Skirty take the blame? I've a good mind not to give you any cream for dinner."

"I was only obeying orders," said Tibbles mournfully. "Us cat-slaves must obey the Purple-Stockings. If you untie me, I'll tell you the whole story."

"Don't!" squeaked Old Noshie. "He'll run away!"

Tibbles groaned. "Oh, the PAIN! These ropes cut into my war wound from the Battle of Fungus Gulch!"

Mr Snelling picked up the kitchen scissors, and looked his cat sternly in the eye.

"I'll untie you," he said, "if you promise not to run away."

"I promise!" said Tibbles.

"You'd better keep that promise," hissed Skirty Marm, "or else practise squeaking like a MOUSE!"

The vicar snipped away the clothes line. Tibbles stretched all his paws, smoothed his tail, and sat up on his hind legs.

"Thank you," he said. "You've only heard the witches' side of things so far. I'm afraid the truth will shock you. Old Noshie and Skirty Marm are two extremely dangerous outlaws, wanted on Witch Island for Robbery with Violence."

"He's LYING!" roared the witches.

"Quiet!" ordered Mr Babbercorn. "Go and stand in the corner beside the fridge until he's finished."

Sulkily, the witches went to stand in the corner.

"You humans have been fooled and bamboozled," Tibbles went on. "These witches are the wicked ones. Our Beloved Queen, Mrs Abercrombie, is very sorry for the trouble they've caused. She wanted to spare you the horrible sight of their capture. But if you let me radio for help, she'll send one of her crack broom squadrons, to take them away immediately."

"AARGH!" shrieked Old Noshie.

Skirty Marm was fuming. "It's a pack of LIES!"

"One more interruption," said Mr Babbercorn, "and I'll stuff tea towels in your mouths. Carry on, Tibbles."

Tibbles, turning towards the vicar, made his voice very purry and sweet. "Surely you trust your little Tibby more than a pair of nasty witches?"

The witches gazed at him fearfully. This cat sounded very convincing. What if the humans believed him?

Mr Snelling said, "Old Noshie and Skirty Marm have proved they are our friends. They are brave and noble – and I won't hear a word against them."

"We're proud to know them," added Mr Babbercorn, making the witches' eyes fill with tears of happiness. "Now, suppose you tell us the real truth?"

Tibbles thoughtfully licked a paw. "It's all too true. The queen sent me here to get Old Noshie and Skirty Marm chucked out of this village. I'm her best cat-slave, and I begged her not to do this. 'Your Majesty,' I said, 'it'll only cause trouble with the humans.' But she was too angry to listen. 'Mendax,' she said (that's my real name), 'Mendax – gallant hero of Fungus Gulch – I want these witches CRUSHED, and tell the humans I'll pay for any damage.'"

"What a stinking great load of rubbish!" Skirty Marm said scornfully. "You weren't at the Battle of Fungus Gulch – you're much too young."

"And if you were Mrs Abercrombie's best cat-slave," Old Noshie said, "we'd have seen you combing her beard at the weekly ceremonies!"

"I'm a Secret Agent," said Tibbles-Mendax.

"Naturally, I keep a low profile."

"Pooh," said Skirty Marm. "I don't believe a word of it! The queen would never waste her best cat on a job like this. I bet you're not important at all. Tell us the truth – or start looking for a mouse hole!"

"All right, all right," the cat said with a snarl. "Before I joined the W.I.S.S., I worked in the palace kitchens."

"Har-har-har!" jeered the witches.

"I was very important!" shouted Mendax. "I was the top pastry chef! I trained in witch cuisine, at the Ecole des Sorcières, in Paris!"

Mr Snelling was trying to look serious, but a smile twitched at his lips.

"Mendax is your real name," he said, "and it seems to suit you. In Latin, 'Mendax' means *liar*."

"You're not on Witch Island now," Mr Babbercorn said kindly. "Don't be afraid of telling us the truth – we won't hurt you."

"*I* might," muttered Skirty Marm.

"Nobody will hurt you," said Mr Snelling, giving the witches a warning look over the top of his glasses.

Mendax was silent for a whole minute. When

he spoke again, his voice was small and sulky.

"I did work in the palace kitchens – that bit was true. But I wasn't a pastry chef. I belonged to a mean old Purple-Stocking called Mrs Wilkins, who did the washing-up. She never paid me, and never gave me anything nice to eat."

He began to sob. It was moving to see the tears rolling down into his whiskers.

"I washed up in that kitchen until last month, when I was sent to prison for stealing bat cake. They said they'd let me out early if I did a little job for the W.I.S.S. I couldn't refuse! You can't imagine how terrible it is on Witch Island now the queen has got the Power Hat again! The cat-slaves are treated more cruelly than ever. And she's put a freeze on stockings!"

"She's WHAT?" yelled Skirty Marm.

"No promotions for a hundred years," Mendax said. "The Red-Stockings stay Red. The Greens stay Green. And that way, the old Purples keep total power. The Greens are miffed – but the Reds are furious."

"She can't do that!" protested Old Noshie. "She can't stop witches getting older!"

"She can," sniffed Mendax. "She can do

pretty well anything now she's got the Hat. Oh, please, please don't send me back! I never knew how nice humans are until I came here! Mrs Wilkins kicks me and beats me and starves me!"

He knelt on the table and clasped his paws pleadingly.

"If you let me stay here, I'll help with the cooking, I'll play chess with Mr Snelling—"

"Good gracious," interrupted the vicar. "Do you play chess?"

"Do I play!" exclaimed Mendax. "I'm a grand master."

The witches rudely blew raspberries.

"Well, all right," Mendax said, "I don't exactly play chess. But I could learn! And I do play Monopoly. Oh, *please* let me stay!"

"If I was you," said Skirty Marm, "I'd send this lying, spying little bag of fur straight back to Witch Island!"

"Certainly not," said Mr Snelling. "He can stay with us, and learn to be good. Just as you did."

"Thank you!" cried Mendax, jumping up to lick the vicar's face. "You won't be sorry – I'll be as good as gold! And I'll try ever so hard not to tell any more lies."

Mr Babbercorn noticed that Old Noshie and Skirty Marm still looked suspicious. It was going to take them a while to trust the spy.

"Mendax," he said, "the first thing you must do is tell everyone in this village that the witches are innocent. I will call a parish meeting, and you will make a public confession."

"It'll be the best confession you ever heard," Mendax assured him.

"That's what I'm afraid of," said Mr Babbercorn. "Just make sure it's a *true* one."

5

Absent Friends

Mendax made his public confession in the village hall. The people of Tranters End were proud of their two local witches, and when they heard that Old Noshie and Skirty Marm were innocent, they burst into loud cheers.

It did not take them long to get used to the vicar's talking cat. In just a few days, they were all saying hello to Mendax when they met him in the street. Everyone liked him because he was extremely polite and obviously trying very hard to behave. He did all the washing-up at the vicarage (except the saucepans which were too heavy for his paws). He cleaned the kitchen floor with a dish mop, which took ages. The vicar gave him a very small shopping basket, and he often popped out to Mrs Tucker's shop. He even baked cakes.

"It's wonderful what he can do with those

little paws," Mr Snelling said happily. "That cat is an absolute treasure."

"Hmmm," said Mr Babbercorn. "I caught him telling the Brownies about how he jumped off the Eiffel Tower for a bet during his student days in Paris. I wish he'd stop those awful *lies*. Then maybe the witches would trust him."

Old Noshie and Skirty Marm did not join in what Skirty called the "Mendax-mania". They had never liked the cat-slaves – those lackeys of the mean old Purple-Stockings – and still thought Mendax a shady character.

"Once a spy, always a spy!" said Skirty Marm darkly.

She was not pleased to find Mendax waiting in the belfry one afternoon. The witches had been out on their broomsticks, usefully clearing leaves out of the vicarage gutters. They flew in through the window, and there was the small black cat, quivering with excitement.

"At last!" he mewed.

Old Noshie and Skirty Marm looked round suspiciously. Mendax was wearing a small flowery apron. The kettle was boiling, and plates of fresh bats and beetles were laid out neatly on the floor.

The witches were tired and hungry, and could not help feeling rather pleased – though Skirty Marm tried to hide it.

She growled, "What's all this in aid of?"

Mendax, standing on his hind legs with his tail tucked over one arm, poured cups of hot rainwater.

"How do you like your water?" he asked. "One spit, or two?"

"Two," said Old Noshie. "Good, big ones – and a spot of dribble. Thanks, Mendax."

She sat down on her cushion, and watched

Mendax spitting daintily into her tea. It smelled delicious, and she had forgotten to be cross with him.

Skirty Marm, however, was not so easily swayed.

"What are you doing here?"

Mendax passed round the plate of bats. "You've got to let me be your friend. I came here with some very important news."

Skirty Marm snorted rudely. "We're not interested in your big, fat LIES."

"I've given up lying," said Mendax.

"No, you haven't," chuckled Old Noshie with her mouth full. "You told Mrs Tucker you saved the queen's life at Fungus Gulch – what a whopper!"

"I *swear*, on the vicar's collar, this is *true*!" cried Mendax. "Oh, witches, please listen! If you care at all about your fellow witches, please trust me! I've had a message for you on my radio set!"

The witches stared. They knew that Mendax still listened to the WBC (Witch Broadcasting Company) on his radio in the garden shed. Could he have picked up a message from the island?

"For *us*?" gasped Old Noshie.

"It was an SOS," Mendax said, tucking the end of his tail into his apron pocket. "Just a frightened sort of voice – 'Calling Old Noshie and Skirty Marm, wherever you are, help, help, help! You are our only hope!' Then there was a shout, and silence."

This certainly sounded like trouble.

Skirty Marm asked, "Who was it?"

"I don't know," said Mendax, "but I tuned into the news, and heard that some Red-Stocking witches had been plotting against the queen. Two of them disguised themselves as Purples, and were caught breaking into the Palace."

This was sensational. Old Noshie and Skirty Marm had been very shocked to hear about the stocking freeze. They were impressed to hear that their old Red-Stocking friends had not taken the monstrous injustice lying down.

"Most of the plotters escaped," Mendax went on, "but they arrested the ringleader – a witch called Badsleeves."

"BADSLEEVES!" choked Old Noshie. "She had the cave next door to ours! Do you remember, Skirt?"

"Of course," said Skirty Marm. "We shared

71

many a bat with dear old Baddy. She was just about the only witch I was sorry to leave behind."

Mendax said, "She got caught when her cave-mate went to the police—"

"SNEEVIL!" yelled Skirty Marm in a sudden rage. "That nasty old bag! Didn't I always tell you, Noshie? Steer clear of that Sneevil, I always said. She told bigger lies than this cat, and she STOLE my best BLOOMERS!"

Witch Island is cold and damp, and witches are very serious about their underwear. Stealing these precious garments is considered very low indeed.

"They were a lovely pair," Old Noshie said, "and you'd just got them soft."

Skirty Marm groaned. "This is terrible! There must be something we can do for poor Badsleeves!"

"Her trial is fixed for tonight," said Mendax. "I thought you might like to listen to it on my radio."

"Come on!" Skirty Marm pulled open the door to the one hundred and eighty-six belfry steps. "Let's tell Mr B. He'll know what to do."

*

It took Mr Babbercorn some time to understand the story – partly because he had two witches and a cat all talking at once, and partly because he found the politics of Witch Island so bewildering.

"Your friend Badsleeves sounds very brave," he said when he had grasped the details. "Is there anything you can do to help her?"

"No," sighed Old Noshie. "Not even if we went back to Witch Island."

"And if they went back there," Mendax said, "they'd be thrown into prison at once. They'd never be so daft."

Skirty Marm was frowning her thinking frown. "If we could go back and help Badsleeves to escape, perhaps we could find the other plotters—"

"Are you BONKERS?" screamed Old Noshie, turning the colour of an old sprout. "You'll get us killed!"

"Fat lot of use you'd be, anyway," said Mendax.

Skirty Marm ignored them, and looked at Mr Babbercorn. "I know it'd be dangerous, and I hate dangerous things. But I can't be happy with myself ever again if I don't try to rescue Badsleeves."

Mr Babbercorn patted her ragged, bony shoulder. "You're a noble witch, Skirty."

"I feel just the same," Old Noshie said quickly. She did not, but fancied being called "noble" by the curate. Besides, if Skirty Marm insisted on going into danger, Old Noshie had to go too. Frightened as she was, there was no question of letting her friend go without her.

Mr Babbercorn's eyes were full of tears. "Splendid witches! But should I let you take such a risk?"

Suddenly, Skirty Marm had a terrible thought.

"You!" she turned to Mendax. "You'd better not be lying! Because if this is a trick to get us chucked into prison—"

"It's the *truth*!" hissed Mendax. "And to prove it, I'll go back to Witch Island with you!"

The witches were thunderstruck.

"But you're a cat-slave!" said Old Noshie. "If you get caught, they'll use you as a brush for cleaning chimneys!"

Mendax looked proud. "I'm tired of you all thinking I can't be trusted. As a matter of fact, I hate Mrs Abercrombie's government as much as you do. You'll find it pretty useful, having a cat-slave on your side."

"All right," growled Skirty Marm, "you can come with us. But no funny business – or else!"

"Or else we'll biff you right into next week," said Old Noshie.

Mendax jumped off the top of the television set, and went towards the kitchen.

"I'll make some sandwiches for the journey."

The short winter's day was nearly over when Old Noshie and Skirty Marm prepared to mount their broomsticks in the vicarage garden. Mr Babbercorn had given them each a pair of his own long woolly pants to keep out the bitter cold. The witches found them superbly comfortable, and wonderfully elegant.

"They're almost as good as my stolen bloomers," Skirty Marm said.

They looked rather funny, sticking out underneath the witches' black rags, but the vicar and the curate felt far too anxious to laugh.

"Good luck," said Mr Babbercorn. "Try to stay out of trouble. Obviously, you must use as much magic as you like. Anything, to save your poor friend and bring justice to Witch Island."

Mendax sat in a basket on the back of Old Noshie's broom, with the smallest saucepan tied on his head as a crash helmet.

"If I don't come back," he said bravely, "please give my duvet to the cat at the post office."

Soft-hearted Mr Snelling was weeping. "Do be careful! I'll miss you all so dreadfully!"

It was a long and difficult ride to Witch Island. Old Noshie and Skirty Marm put on their goggles and muttered the revving-up spell to start their brooms. Skirty Marm checked the

switches on the broom handles, which enabled them to talk to each other while flying.

"Contact!" she cried. "Set course for W.I.!" And the two brooms zoomed off into the darkening sky.

The night was freezing, and the cold became mixed with a terrible dampness as they approached Witch Island. The old home of the witches and Mendax looked very black and bleak when the two brooms landed on the sooty palace beach. The air was damp and chilly with sea spray, and smelled of bad eggs.

"So far, so good," said Skirty Marm. "Not a soul about. They must all be packed into the Meeting Cave."

"Let's have our sandwiches," suggested Old Noshie. She stuffed a mouse roll into her mouth.

"Put those away!" snapped Skirty Marm. "We need to find a way into that Meeting Cave without being seen."

"That's impossible!" cried Old Noshie. "And I refuse to be killed and stuffed and put in the queen's trophy room, until I've finished my picnic!"

"Quiet," said Skirty Marm. "I'm thinking."

She wriggled her fingers and toes. The smelly

air of her old home made her tingle with inspiration.

"Of course!" she said. "Mendax, you're a cat-slave. You can sneak us in through the cats' alley!"

Mendax had gone very quiet. He was trembling, from the ends of his whiskers to the tip of his tail.

"I was afraid you'd think of that," he said. He took off his saucepan helmet. "You'd better follow me. Leave the brooms under this big rock. And the sandwiches."

"Drat," grumbled Old Noshie. "I'm starving!"

They hid the broomsticks and sandwiches. Putting his paw to his mouth, Mendax led the witches through a hidden opening in the massive black rock, and into a dark, winding tunnel. It was one of the tunnels built specially for cat-slaves, and very cramped. Old Noshie and Skirty Marm had to crawl on their hands and knees.

"Ow!" complained Old Noshie, who was rather plump, "My bottom keeps getting stuck! And these rocks will wear out our new long johns."

"Shhh!" hissed Skirty Marm. "Or some

78

stinky cat-slave will hear us and give us away to the Purples!"

"No offence, Mendax," said Old Noshie.

"Hmph!" snorted Skirty Marm. She was annoyed that her friend found it so easy to be nice to the spy.

The crawl along the cats' alley was very uncomfortable, and seemed to take ages. At last, they saw a light at the tunnel's end. It grew brighter, and suddenly the two witches found themselves peering through a small opening, high up in the wall of the Meeting Cave.

"Wow!" gasped Old Noshie.

It was an incredible sight. The huge Meeting Cave was seething with every witch on the island – from ancient Purple-Stockings of five and six hundred years old, to baby Yellows of only seventy or eighty. On the high platform stood the enormous granite throne of Mrs Abercrombie. The stone walls echoes with the shrieks and shouts of thousands of witches fighting for the best seats.

A public trial was a great event on Witch Island, and everyone was in a holiday mood. Around the feet of the crowd ran dozens of cat-slaves with trays of snacks and drinks.

"The lower class of cat," whispered Mendax. "They belong to the Purples who have food licences, poor creatures."

Old Noshie and Skirty Marm were not interested in the cat-slaves. They were staring down at their old comrades, the Red-Stockings. These young witches – all under suspicion because of the plot – sat in a special section of the cave, looking very sulky, and surrounded by police witches.

"They all hate the stocking freeze," Skirty Marm said. "It's all right for the Greens – they have enough power to keep them satisfied. But who wants to stay a Red with smelly old Greens and Purples telling you what to do? It's a scandal! It's an insult! Shall the Red-Stockings accept defeat? No!"

"Stop making speeches!" Old Noshie whispered crossly. "What are we going to do now?"

They were in terrible danger. As soon as one of the busy witches below them thought of looking up, they would be discovered and arrested.

"Well, it's impossible," said Old Noshie. "Let's go home."

Skirty Marm, fingers crossed, mumbled a spell.

"Help!" squealed Old Noshie. "I feel funny . . . something's happening to my legs . . ."

Her voice trailed off into a long miaow. Her black rags and new long johns turned into black, silky fur. Before her astonished eyes, her hands and feet changed into paws.

"Good gracious!" said Mendax.

"I don't like it!" mewed the cat who was Old Noshie. "We'll get trodden on!"

"Now you know how it feels to be a helpless slave," said Mendax.

Skirty Marm picked up her new tail and gazed at it, fascinated. "I don't know what you lot find to compain about. This feels great."

"Just wait!" Mendax said darkly. "Wait till some old Purple kicks you with her smelly fat foot and sends you off to work in the sulphur mines!"

"Blimey," muttered Old Noshie, "aren't these whiskers *itchy*?"

Now that they were cats, they could easily run down the narrow ledge of rock, to the heart of the Meeting Cave. As Skirty Marm had hoped, none of the excited witches took any notice of three more cat-slaves.

"But we've got to get proper disguises, before someone notices we don't belong to anyone," said Mendax. "Come on – I'll show you how to behave. I don't suppose either of you know a decent sleeping spell?"

"No!" quavered Old Noshie. "Let's go home!"

"Shut up, you coward!" mewed Skirty Marm. Red sparks flew from the ends of her whiskers. "Of course I know a sleeping spell! Get on with it, Mendax – and less of your cheek!"

She did not like taking orders from a cat, but knew that she had no choice. The two friends followed Mendax through a small, cat-sized door in the mossy wall of the cave. Behind it, they found three cat-slaves, refilling their trays of food and drink from a large box. An ugly Purple-Stocking stood over them with a cat whip.

"Hurry up!" she growled. "Move those paws!"

Skirty Marm mumbled the sleeping spell (always one of her best). The Purple-Stocking witch and her three cat-slaves instantly fell into a deep sleep.

"Right," said Mendax over the snores of the

Purple. "Stand up on your back legs, put the trays round your necks, do what I do . . . and don't be too polite to the Red-Stockings."

Old Noshie and Skirty Marm put on their trays – with some difficulty, because they were not used to having paws instead of hands. Mendax had to show Old Noshie how to put her tail over one arm so it would not trip her up. At last, their disguise was complete.

Mendax strolled back into the Meeting Cave, mewing at the top of his voice, "Pond sludge! Fried weasel! Newt skulls! Get your snacks here!"

"Snacks!" mewed the witches bravely. "Get your lovely snacks here!"

It was awful to be so small among so many fierce Purple- and Green-Stockings. Old Noshie and Skirty Marm did not dare to look around, but kept their eyes fixed on Mendax's back.

"Oi! Cat!" yelled a nasty voice. A wrinkled hand shot out of the crowd and grabbed Mendax by the ear. It belonged to a Green-Stocking. "Fried weasel – and be quick about it!"

Mendax handed over a weasel, and took the Green-Stocking's money.

"Tut tut," he said. "Haven't you got the right change?"

"None of your lip!" screamed the Green-Stocking. "Don't you see the colour of these stockings?"

Skirty Marm glanced up at the witch's face, and let out a sudden spit of fury.

"Look!" she whispered to the cat who was Old Noshie, "That's no Green! It's SNEEVIL! The queen must have promoted her as a reward for betraying Badsleeves! Oh, wouldn't I love to squash her nose?"

Old Noshie gulped. The Green-Stocking was indeed the wicked Sneevil who had once shared the cave next to theirs.

Skirty Marm dropped to the floor, just long enough to look up Sneevil's dress.

"I knew it!" she hissed. "She's wearing them!"

"Shut up about your bloomers," groaned Old Noshie, "or you'll ruin everything!"

Mendax had counted out Sneevil's change. He nodded to the witches, and they followed him through the crowd. Several times, witches stopped them to buy snacks. Old Noshie and Skirty Marm were very shocked by the rude way the older witches spoke to cat-slaves. After twenty minutes, their sides were black and blue from kicks and pinches.

"I know," said Mendax, seeing their faces. "You're not the only ones who want a revolution."

He settled them inside a dip in the cave wall, with a beautiful view of the platform. They were just a few metres above the dock, where Badsleeves would soon be standing. They could not forget that they had once stood there themselves, on the terrible day of their trial for singing the rude song about Mrs Abercrombie.

"Poor Badsleeves," said Old Noshie, "I know how she must be feeling."

Suddenly, there was a deafening fanfare of trumpets.

"Look out," said Skirty Marm. "Here comes Mrs Stinkbomb, our glorious queen."

6

S·L·A·W·

A great silence fell upon the Meeting Cave. Two ceremonial cat-slaves, wearing collars of gold, marched onto the platform and stood on either side of the massive stone throne.

In stomped the Queen of all the Witches, Mrs Abercrombie. Her red eyes glittered meanly in her ugly face. Her iron teeth gleamed, and her grey beard shot out sparks of fury. Her gigantic body dropped down on the throne, with a mighty "plop".

Every witch in the cave – including the sulky Red-Stockings – bowed until their noses touched the floor. They were all terrified of Mrs Abercrombie. Upon her horrible head, she wore the Power Hat. It was as black and gleaming as a piece of coal, and it stood two metres high. The everlasting candle in its point burned with a bright white stillness.

This was the magic hat Skirty Marm had thrown into the sea, thinking it would end the Queen's cruel reign. She had not known that Mrs Abercrombie's magic would be strong enough to call it back. Was there any place on earth that her magic could not reach? Without the hat, she was brilliant. With it, she was invincible.

"BRING IN THE PRISONER!" she thundered, in a voice that made the walls vibrate.

Old Noshie and Skirty Marm looked down from their hiding place above the dock, impatient to see Badsleeves. Instead, to their surprise, they saw only a police witch carrying a jam jar. The jam jar was filled with greenish water.

"I was too ANGRY to sit through a whole trial," roared Mrs Abercrombie. "I am going to find her guilty anyway – so why waste time?"

She pointed a meaty, accusing finger at the jam jar.

"My subjects, behold the criminal, BADSLEEVES – or what's left of her. I've turned her into a little piece of pond slime. And let this be a warning to all who plot against my sacred person!"

"WOE!" yelled all the witches. "WOE to the TRAITOR!"

The applause crashed on for several m...
The witches cheered and whistled and sta...
their feet. The baby Yellow-Stockings wa...
black flags and hideous photographs of their
queen. The police witches watched the Red-
Stockings to make sure they clapped hard enough.

Mrs Abercrombie (with a satisfied smirk that
did not improve her face) signalled for silence.

"Badsleeves will have plenty of time to accept
my government. I have sentenced her to FIVE
HUNDRED YEARS at the bottom of the
palace pond."

"Hurrah! Hurrah!" cheered all the witches.
"Long live Mrs Abercrombie!"

The queen's hairy face blackened in a
disgusting scowl.

"And you cocky little Red-Stockings – so
pleased with yourselves for opposing ME – since
you fancy yourselves so much, you can stay Red-
Stockings until I get my temper back!"

A great groan of outrage went up from the
Red-Stockings.

"Well, that's that," sighed Old Noshie.
"There's nothing we can do for poor Badsleeves
now. Let's go home."

The words were hardly out of her mouth

when the Meeting Cave was suddenly rocked by a tremendous explosion. A cloud of bright red smoke billowed up from the floor, filling the whole cave with scarlet fog.

In the second of horrified silence that followed, a voice shouted, "Justice for Red-Stockings! Down with the government!"

The cave erupted in confusion and pandemonium. As the fog spread, witches screamed and coughed, and surged towards the exits. Mrs Abercrombie was rushed away through a trap-door in the platform by her hand-picked guard of beefy Purples.

Old Noshie and Skirty Marm stared, open-mouthed, until Mendax nudged them hard.

"Quick!" he mewed above the din. "Now's your chance!"

Seeing at once what he meant, the two disguised witches leapt down into the dock. Skirty Marm gabbled a spell that turned them both back into witches. Old Noshie biffed the police witch, who was too shocked to defend herself. Skirty Marm grabbed the jar of pond slime that was Badsleeves.

Just as she was gazing wildly around, wondering what on earth to do next, she felt the paws of Mendax landing on her shoulder.

"The door!" he purred against her ear. "Through the door! I know a way out!"

There was a door at the back of the dock, which led to a bare corridor (Skirty and Noshie dimly remembered being led down it, in hand-cuffs, on the day of their own trial). The witches and Mendax dived through this door, and dashed off down the corridor. Three fierce police witches dashed after them. Noshie and Skirty biffed right and left, until two of the police witches lay stunned at their feet with their hats pulled down over their faces.

"Nice work, Nosh!" shouted Skirty Marm.

Mendax was sitting on the head of the third police witch. He bit her ear, and she ran away down the corridor, blowing her whistle for help.

A second later, the corridor echoed with the sound of approaching police boots.

Old Noshie flew into a panic, and grabbed the back of Skirty Marm's ragged black dress. A large part of it ripped away in her hand, and Skirty reacted by biffing her friend's nose.

"You clumsy moron!" she shouted. "I've been working on these rags for years!"

"I couldn't help it!" roared Old Noshie.

Round the bend in the corridor, voices bellowed, "Stop! In the name of the queen!"

Unlike the witches, Mendax had stayed calm. He was feeling along the wall, near the floor. His clever paws pressed something, and a section of the wall swung open. The door was very small, but there was no time for Noshie and Skirty to change themselves back into cats. They dived through the small door, and it clanged shut behind them.

They were suddenly in total silence and total darkness. Skirty Marm lit the end of her finger (witches can easily do this without hurting themselves) and held up the flame. Its reflection shone dully on the close, damp walls.

"Where are we?" she asked.

Mendax's eyes gleamed like emeralds in the eerie light.

"I've let you into a secret cat tunnel," he said. "The island's full of them, but this is the first time a witch has ever been inside. If the other cats get to hear about this, I'll be thrown to the sharks."

Skirty Marm cleared her throat. She hated apologizing, but this needed to be said.

"Mendax, I'm sorry I've been horrid to you.

You saved our lives just now. You are on our side, after all. Please forgive me for not trusting you."

Mendax beamed happily. "Don't mention it. After all, we didn't meet in the best circumstances." He held out his paw, and the witches both shook it.

Skirty Marm checked the jam jar.

"You saved Badsleeves, too," she said, peering into the greenish water. "I hope we haven't spilled her."

"Can you change her back, Skirt?" Old Noshie asked anxiously.

Skirty Marm did not like admitting there were things she could not do, but she had to shake her head. "This spell is far too tough for me to budge. It would take a Purple-Stocking, at least."

"I wonder if she can hear us in there?" said Old Noshie. She leaned closer to the jar. "Hello, Baddy. It's Old Noshie – remember me? We're being chased by the police and we'll probably end up getting killed, but we don't want you to worry."

"Fat lot of comfort you are!" Skirty Marm said scornfully. She was still very angry about her torn rags. She shone her flaming finger around the blackness. "I wish I knew where we were. Mendax, where does this secret tunnel of yours come out?"

Mendax wrinkled his nose. "The sewers."

The witches cried, "Oh, BLEUCHH!"

Few sewers are pleasant places, but the sewers of Witch Island are more disgusting than you can possibly imagine. Even the most hardened old Purples, who usually like a bit of filth, refuse to go down there. All maintenance work is carried out by cat-slaves who don't have any choice.

"Well, that's done it," said Skirty Marm. Her voice was gloomy. "There are hundreds of miles of sewers. We could be lost in here for years."

"Ahem," said Mendax. He looked unhappy. "I happen to know my way around."

"This is no time for one of your lies!" snapped Old Noshie.

Mendax sighed. "I'm not lying. I used to work in the sewers when Mrs Wilkins was Effluent Manager."

The witches gasped. A sewer was the last place you would expect to find an elegant cat like Mendax.

"You said she worked in the palace kitchen . . ." faltered Old Noshie.

"She did – afterwards," Mendax said with a shudder. "Believe it or not, washing dishes was regarded as a promotion. To be honest, I preferred the sewers. I didn't have to see so much of Mrs Wilkins."

Old Noshie stroked his smooth back kindly. "Poor Mendax, you had a horrid life on this island."

His green eyes flooded with tears. "You cannot imagine," he said, "the degradation of being the cat-slave of a low-class Purple like Mrs Wilkins. Can you wonder that I dislike the truth?" He shuddered again. "She won me in a game of ping-pong when I was a kitten. She kicked me, she starved me – she got drunk and sent me down to the Nasty Medicine shop with the empties. A cat of my calibre . . . But enough of this." Mendax coughed, and proudly raised his head. "Let us proceed."

On their hands and knees, Old Noshie and Skirty Marm began to crawl along the secret tunnel. It was hard, unpleasant work. Skirty Marm held up her lighted finger. Old Noshie carried the jam jar very carefully, sometimes

saying a comforting word or two to Badsleeves.

At last, after nearly an hour of this, the cat tunnel stopped short at a stone door.

"This will take us into the main sewer," said Mendax. "There's a lot of gas down there, and we don't want another explosion. You'd better put out that finger."

"Not to worry, Badsleeves," Old Noshie told the jar. "Your pond water will get calmer in a minute, when I can stand up."

Skirty Marm blew out the flame at the tip of her finger. For a moment, they were plunged back into blackness. Then the low door opened and they emerged into a far bigger tunnel – dim and dripping, with a thick stream oozing between the brick banks. The smell was amazingly disgusting. Mendax's eyes watered, and he staggered backwards.

"Bit whiffy in here," remarked Old Noshie.

"It is rather strong," agreed Skirty Marm.

There was a cramped stone path beside the sluggish stream. Every twenty metres or so it widened into a deep bay. The faint, sickly light came from lamps set into the slimy walls.

"I think—" began Mendax.

Nobody ever knew what he thought. Before he could finish the sentence, something grabbed him from behind and clamped a dirty hand across his mouth.

At the same moment two witches, their faces hidden by black masks, jumped on Old Noshie and Skirty Marm.

It is difficult to know where you are going, when your hands are tied and you are wearing a blindfold. By the time the masked witches had stopped pulling and shoving, Noshie and Skirty were exhausted.

Rough hands pushed them down on a hard, cold floor.

A stern voice growled, "Take off their blindfolds!"

The blindfolds were untied, and Old Noshie and Skirty Marm blinked as they gazed around. They seemed to be in one of the deep brick bays beside the main sewer. The shadows were studded with dozens of pairs of gleaming eyes. Skirty Marm looked from the eyes down to the legs below. In the dim light, she saw something that made her break into a broad smile.

"You're Red-Stockings!" she shouted. "Oh, this is just like old times! What are you doing down here?"

"We ask the questions," growled the voice. "Who are you working for?"

"The police, I bet," someone said. "I vote we give them a good bashing."

"Well, I'll be blowed," said Skirty Marm, staring hard at the first speaker. "It's Binbag!"

And the Red-Stocking called Binbag gasped, "Blimey, it's Skirty Marm! And the other's Old Noshie – I'd know that vacant green face anywhere!"

This caused a sensation. There were shouts

and cheers. Noshie and Skirty were untied, and thirty beaming witches tried to shake their hands and slap them on the back.

Binbag had been at school with Old Noshie and Skirty Marm, and a great grin was plastered across her toothless face.

"Our heroines!" she cried. "You heard our radio message, and you came to help us!"

"Oh, that was you, was it?" said Old Noshie. She had made up her mind to be very cross about being kidnapped, but couldn't help liking the word "heroines".

Binbag swelled importantly. "This is our secret hideout. We are the S.L.A.W." She added, "That stands for the Secret Liberation Army of Witches. We were going to call ourselves Red-Stockings Against the Stocking Freeze, but that didn't make such a nice word. It was us who hatched that plot against Mrs Abercrombie – and us who made that lovely explosion at the trial. Now we're outlaws, and the whole island is looking for us. That's why we have to hide down here." She stood up. "But we will never surrender! We're going to knock Mrs A. off her throne, once and for all!"

She began to sing:

"Witches arise, at the break of the dawn!
March to the celebration!
Make Mrs A. wish she'd never been born,
O Army of Witch Liberation!"

One by one, the other witches took up the song, until the whole sewer rang with it.

"Spirits of Noshie and Skirty Marm,
Inspire us in our endeavour!
Biff them and bash them – but keep us from harm,
You who are so bold and clever!"

"There's twenty-three more verses," said Binbag.

"I liked the bit about us," said Old Noshie, who was not often called "clever".

"You two are legends among us Red-Stockings," Binbag told her. "When you were first banished, we thought you were dead. Then you came back and chucked the Power Hat into the sea. Now we need your help again."

"Wait!" Skirty Marm cried suddenly. "Where's Mendax?"

"Who? Oh, you mean that cat." Binbag

pointed to a sack on the floor. It was squirming and uttering stifled mews.

Noshie and Skirty rushed to let Mendax out and untie his gag. They had forgotten him because they had been too busy basking in compliments, and now they felt very guilty.

"You beasts!" said Old Noshie. "You've rumpled his whiskers!"

All the other witches had shrunk back against the slimy wall. As far as they knew, all cat-slaves were the tools of the enemy. Skirty Marm saw that she had to introduce this particular cat properly.

"Listen, you lot," she said. "This is Mendax, and he's a friend of ours. He saved our lives today. He showed us that the cat-slaves are only mean to us because the oldies treat them so badly. They want to be free. We won't help your S.L.A.W. unless you promise to free the cat-slaves!"

"Hear! hear," said Mendax, smoothing his squashed whiskers.

"I suppose so," Binbag said doubtfully. "If they all promise to vote for Badsleeves when we have our first election."

"Badsleeves!" choked Old Noshie and Skirty

Marm, suddenly remembering the jar of pond slime.

"Oh dear," said Mendax.

"She was in that jam jar," whispered Old Noshie. "Did you happen to save it?"

To her great surprise, the S.L.A.W. witches giggled.

"It fell in the water," said Binbag. The other witches giggled harder.

"You old fools!" yelled Skirty Marm. "You've just thrown your leader into the sewer!"

"Hello, Skirt," said a familiar voice. "Hello, Noshie."

To the amazement of Old Noshie and Skirty Marm, out of the shadows stepped their old friend and neighbour, Badsleeves. She was a short, stout witch, with sticking-up white hair and round glasses. She chuckled, when she saw their shocked faces.

"Binbag stole an Advanced Purple Spell-book," she explained. "I was smuggled out of prison on the bottom of her shoe, and she changed me back into a witch just before the trial. There was nothing in that jam jar of yours except ordinary pond slime. From a pond."

"Huh," Old Noshie muttered crossly. "I

needn't have tried to cheer it up!"

"Sorry, Noshie," said Badsleeves. "It was really kind of you." She gazed at them solemnly, through her little round glasses. "And I'm afraid I have to ask you to do something else for us."

Old Noshie and Skirty Marm, remembering that they were legends and heroines with a song about them, cried, "Anything!"

"All of us in this sewer are marked witches," said Badsleeves. "The minute we show ourselves, we'll be arrested. But nobody knows you two are on the island. That means you won't show up on the queen's radar. So we need you to sneak past the palace guards, and steal back the Power Hat."

The two Legends squealed.

"Oh, that's ALL, is it?" shouted Skirty Marm sarcastically. "ALL we have to do is steal the Power Hat? Well, pooh to you – you always were a BARMY sort of witch."

"I bet the queen never takes that hat off for a single minute," said Old Noshie. "Not after last time. I bet she's guarded round the clock. We wouldn't stand a chance!"

"True," said Badsleeves. "The Hat is heavily guarded at all times."

Skirty Marm was unhappy. She did not enjoy disappointing her fans by letting S.L.A.W. down.

"We'd help you if there was any way at all," she said. "But don't you see? It's IMPOSSIBLE!"

"Ahem," said Mendax.

Everyone turned to look at him. He coolly licked his paw.

"May I make a suggestion?"

7

A Good Clean Fight

"Here is the problem," Mendax said. "If you don't knock Mrs Abercrombie off her throne, you lot will have to hide in the sewers for ever. You can't get rid of Mrs Abercrombie, unless you get hold of the Power Hat. And you'll never get the Power Hat unless you can sneak past her guards."

All the witches nodded sadly. It looked hopeless.

"But there is a chance," the intelligent cat went on. "There is one time of day when the queen is totally ALONE. And that is when—"

"When she takes her BATH!" interrupted Badsleeves. "Don't be ridiculous, cat. How are we supposed to sneak into the queen's bathroom? Why, she has ten of her biggest, meanest guards outside the door!"

"It'll be risky," Mendax said, "but I'm sure

it can be done. Listen . . ."

Quietly and calmly, he outlined his bold plan. Old Noshie and Skirty Marm were horrified as they heard what they were supposed to do – apart from anything else, the idea of Mrs Abercrombie without any clothes on made them feel quite faint. But the S.L.A.W. were relying on them, and they could not let their friends down now.

"Very well," said Badsleeves when Mendax had finished. "If you can do the dangerous part, we'll do the rest."

She shook hands with Old Noshie and Skirty Marm, and also shook the paw of Mendax.

"Goodbye," she said. "And thank you. Witch Island will never forget your courage."

"I may write another verse about you for our song," piped up Binbag. "So goodbye, and don't worry that it's all been for nothing."

"Why do you keep saying goodbye?" Old Noshie demanded crossly. "Don't you want to see us again?"

There was an embarrassed silence.

"Of course, we *want* to see you again," said Badsleeves. "It's just that we probably won't."

"I hope it's not too painful," said Binbag.

"Look on the bright side. She might do it quickly."

"Remember!" cried Badsleeves. "You'll be making history! Your glorious names will live for ever!"

"Hmm," muttered Skirty Marm, "I'd just like my glorious body to live until tomorrow, thanks."

Binbag slapped her on the back. "When it's all over, we'll give you a lovely funeral— I mean, party."

Not surprisingly, when Old Noshie and Skirty Marm set off along the sewer on their mission, they were very depressed.

"Well, this is a nice mess," said Skirty Marm.

"Mr Babbercorn will miss us," sniffed Old Noshie.

"Brace up, witches!" said Mendax. "I remember at Fungus Gulch, when I was about to lead my lads in that last, desperate attack on Bendy Ridge—"

"SHUT UP!" roared both the witches.

"Sorry," sighed Mendax. "I was only lying to keep my spirits up."

Mendax was leading, for they were headed for the palace kitchens where he had once worked. There was a cat-slaves' alley joining it to the sewers. Once again, Old Noshie and Skirty Marm had to squeeze themselves through a damp, narrow tunnel. By now, their elbows were covered in grazes and their black rags had run into dozens of new holes. Curiously, however, the long johns given by Mr Babbercorn remained as good as new.

"If a witch got herself a few pairs of these and sold them on this island," Skirty Marm said, "she'd make her fortune."

"Here we are," whispered Mendax. He was trembling all over. "Oh, what ghastly memories come surging back! What endless nights of whipping and biffing!"

From the other side of the cats' door, Old Noshie and Skirty Marm heard the sounds of the busy kitchen – pans clanking, crockery rattling, loud voices and running footsteps. Mrs Abercrombie's appetite was huge, and so were the appetites of her hand-picked guards. The palace kitchens were never idle.

Mendax curled himself round Old Noshie's neck like a black scarf, and hid under her rags.

He whispered ticklish instructions into her ear. "Open the door . . . keep your heads

108

down . . . turn right at the cupboard marked 'Overalls' . . ."

The two witches obeyed him, with their hearts in their mouths. It was ghastly to plunge into a huge, smoky, steamy kitchen full of dangerous old Greens and Purples. On one side of the room was a great fire, where chefs and cat-slaves worked around bubbling cauldrons, stirring, frying and basting. Cat-slaves with trays tied to their backs ran to and fro with stacks of dirty plates.

"The Bath Snack is being prepared," whispered Mendax. "One trolley for the queen, and five for the guardroom. Get yourselves some overalls, for goodness' sake."

The overall cupboard was covered with notices. "Protective Clothing to be Worn at All Times." "No Singing." "Do Not Kill Cat-Slaves near Royal Food." Doing their best to look casual, Old Noshie and Skirty Marm put on big white aprons and tall white hats. Old Noshie pulled her hat down low, to hide her green face.

"That's the one," whispered Mendax. "The huge trolley near the sink."

The sink was the size of a small swimming pool. A crowd of cat-slaves were busily washing dishes around it. Their fur was soaking wet and covered with blobs of old food. Their paws were cracked and swollen.

This was where Mendax had worked. Old Noshie heard a sob in her ear, and wished she dared to say something comforting. She and Skirty Marm had never dreamed that the mysterious cat-slaves could be treated so cruelly.

A truly revolting old Purple-Stocking, reeking of Nasty Medicine, stood over the sink with a cat whip. Every few minutes, she shouted, "Faster!" and brought her whip down on a cat's back.

"That's Mrs Wilkins," whispered Mendax. "Drunk, as usual."

"Smelly old beast!" Skirty Marm said in a kind of whispered growl. "Don't worry, Mendax – we'll set your friends free. I'm so angry now, I'm not even scared!"

"Well, I'm terrified," said Old Noshie. "I'm so terrified that my tummy keeps gurgling."

The queen's snack trolley was enormous, and heaped with covered dishes. It wafted out a strong smell of baked bat, which made Old Noshie's stomach gurgle worse than ever. A bell rang so loudly that the big saucepans on the walls shook like the church bells of Tranters End. Two large Green-Stocking under-chefs kicked their way through the cat-slaves, and pushed the Royal trolley out of the kitchen.

"Go on!" hissed Mendax. "You've got five minutes before the other trolleys leave!"

Very scared, Old Noshie and Skirty Marm scuttled after the queen's Bath Snack. Skirty Marm managed to pick up a heavy ladle without being noticed by the bustling kitchen witches.

"Don't biff until you see the reds of their eyes!" she whispered.

Skirty Marm rather liked a good fight. Old

Noshie did not, and she was shaking like a jelly.

"This is crazy!" she squeaked. "They're HUGE!"

The rocky corridor outside the kitchen was deserted. It was now or never – this was the window of opportunity upon which Mendax had based his plan. He tightened his paws round Old Noshie's neck. Skirty Marm swung her ladle, and dealt the biggest trolley witch a handsome wallop. Old Noshie jumped at the other one, but was not fast enough. The angry Green-Stocking pulled a switch in the stone wall.

"Whoops," said Mendax.

A door opened in the wall. There was a rushing sound, and out zoomed two armoured broomsticks without riders.

"You're finished!" screamed one of the Green-Stockings. "You're going straight to prison!"

"No, we're not!" cried Skirty Marm. To Old Noshie's surprise, she held up her hand, and shouted, "Brooms! Set 'em off, brooms!"

To Noshie's greater surprise, the two armoured broomsticks suddenly changed direction and jumped on the two Green-Stockings. Automatic handcuffs shot out of their brushes. In a very few minutes, they had cuffed the two roaring, spitting Greens and bundled them through a very smelly flap in the wall near by.

"The rubbish chute," said Mendax with a purr of satisfaction. "How very appropriate."

"But how?" gasped Old Noshie.

"Don't you recognize them?" Skirty Marm chuckled. "Our old brooms! The ones who left us when we got to Tranters End! They've been retrained – but they haven't forgotten us!" She patted both broomsticks. "Thanks, brooms. As you were."

The two broomsticks glided serenely away.

"Quick!" mewed Mendax.

Old Noshie whipped the cover off one of the dishes on the trolley – a selection of cold bats, mice and porcupines. Mendax jumped onto the plate.

"Cor," said Old Noshie, "doesn't it smell lovely?"

She replaced the cover. Now it was time for the hardest part. The witches began to push the trolley towards the Royal bathroom.

A very big Purple-Stocking – one of Mrs Abercrombie's elite guards – stood outside the entrance to the queen's private suite.

Skirty Marm and Old Noshie were trembling with terror when they pushed the trolley past her. But all she said was, "Hurry up with those snacks – she's in a horrible temper."

Echoing through the underground caves, a dreadful voice bellowed, "WHERE'S MY SNACK?"

Only a few metres to the bathroom – but it was the longest walk of the witches' lives. Never had their belfry seemed so safe and cosy. Keeping their heads well down, they had to push the trolley through the outer room full of guards. The red badges on the guards' pointed hats marked them out as the most vicious witches on the island.

One of them pushed open the door to the queen's bathroom.

"ABOUT TIME!" grumbled Mrs Abercrombie. "Keep me waiting again, and it's SEWER DUTY for the lot of you!"

The bathroom was full of steam. Through the damp clouds they could make out a huge stone bath. In this, the Queen of the Witches lay, like a great, wobbly whale. Her mottled purple body was naked except for her Power Hat. The everlasting candle in its point gleamed through the steam with a cold, white radiance. Mrs Abercrombie was scrubbing under her arms with a soapy hedgehog.

"I'll start with a dish of sugared newts," she said.

Old Noshie and Skirty Marm picked up the largest dish, carried it between them to the edge of the bath, and took off the cover.

"AARGH!" bellowed Mrs Abercrombie.

Mendax leapt out like a streak of black lightning, and sank his claws into the Power

Hat. The queen pulled him off and threw him into the water. This gave the two witches just enough time to grab at the Power Hat and wrap their arms around it. It tingled and fizzed with magic.

"GUARDS!" roared Mrs Abercrombie.

Noshie and Skirty pulled with all their might. The Hat was stuck firmly to the Royal head – but Skirty Marm's great anger gave her strength. With a mighty effort, she managed to prise it off. It toppled into the deep, murky water where poor Mendax was struggling to keep his nose above the surface.

"Don't – let – her – get – it – back!" he gasped.

Four guards burst into the bathroom.

"Don't just stand there!" shouted the queen. "Call this security? You're all fired!"

Dropping the hedgehog, she pointed a finger each at Old Noshie and Skirty Marm, and spat out a spell.

At that moment, the witches gave themselves up for lost and prepared to be turned into slugs, pond slime, or another of the queen's favourite punishments.

But nothing happened. The four guards screamed. Old Noshie and Skirty Marm gaped in astonishment. Never before had one of the queen's spells failed.

"Drat," swore Mrs Abercrombie. "They're under some kind of protection and I can't shift it!" She peered through the steam. "It's those long pants. Get them off."

"Mr Babbercorn's long johns!" cried Skirty Marm. "Don't you see, Nosh? They've been worn by a human curate, and now she can't touch us!"

"We'll see about that!" snarled Mrs Abercrombie. The Power Hat lay at the bottom of the bath, beside the queen's mighty behind. Its everlasting candle gleaming eerily under the water. The queen popped a bar of soap into her mouth, and made a grab for the Hat. "I don't care if *all* your underwear belongs to the Archbishop of Canterbury – it's powerless against my Hat!"

Mendax was too quick for her. He drew a deep breath, and dived under the water. When Mrs Abercrombie pulled the Power Hat out of the water, she gave her first scream of real fear – the little cat had crawled inside it, and was clinging to it like a burr. The furious queen shook it and banged it against the wall, but she could not dislodge him.

Now there were three witches and a cat in the bath, punching and swiping and sending up great fountains of water.

Noshie and Skirty fought with all their might, slithering against the queen's soapy body. Every time she tried to climb out of the bath, they jumped on her head and forced her back. Every time the guards advanced, Mendax's voice mewed bravely from inside the Power Hat, "Back – or I'll turn you all into slugs!" As long as his small head was in that hat, he was invincible. Not even the super-magic of the queen could harm him.

His mews were becoming fainter. The grip of his claws was loosening. Old Noshie and Skirty Marm splashed and biffed, and still Mrs Abercrombie brushed them off as if they were flies. But at last Skirty Marm got the Power Hat on her own head – with the sodden, exhausted Mendax still lying, half drowned, inside it.

The guards immediately bowed low. Mrs Abercrombie was a witch of brilliance – but whoever wore the Hat was the strongest witch in the world and rightful Queen of the Island. Her hideous face turned deathly pale.

Crossing her fingers, Skirty Marm muttered a spell.

A pinkish ooze surged out of the overflow in the bath. It spread across the water, and formed a sticky puddle around Mrs Abercrombie. There was a puff of smoke, and the ooze changed into Badsleeves and her Secret Liberation Army.

Mrs Abercrombie screeched and swore. She changed the army into slugs – but with the Hat on her head Skirty Marm could change them back with a single thought.

"You might as well give up!" said Badsleeves. "It'll soon be all over the island – the Reds have grabbed control of the Power Hat! If you want to be in charge again, you'll have to get yourself fairly and squarely elected! Now get out, and find yourself a cave. We're taking over your palace!"

Mrs Abercrombie, with a face of thunder, climbed out of the bath.

"Yuck!" cried Binbag, watching the soapy water sliding off her gigantic, wobbly body.

Badsleeves grinned. "Take her away. Don't worry if she tries any tricks – we've got the Hat."

"You'll pay for this!" rumbled Mrs

Abercrombie. "My Green and Purple subjects will stay loyal to me!"

Old Noshie had begun to eat the Royal Bath Snacks. "I wouldn't count on it!" she chuckled, with her mouth full of newts. Mrs Abercrombie's guards were meekly allowing the Liberation Army to push and prod them out of the crowded bathroom.

Mrs Abercrombie covered her unsavoury nakedness with an enormous grey towel. Distantly, they could all hear cheers, as news of her defeat spread across the island.

"Old Noshie and Skirty Marm," she growled, glaring at the witches, "I'll have my REVENGE on you two, if it's the last thing I do!"

Skirty Marm closed her eyes. Because the Power Hat was on her head, she saw green letters, rather like the letters on a computer screen. *Options*, said the letters. *1. Kill. 2. Squash. 3. Let her go, because you don't really care.*

Number three, thought Skirty Marm. And Mrs Abercrombie, fuming and dripping, was led away by victorious Red-Stockings.

"Well done!" cried Badsleeves. "You can give me the Hat now."

"Not so fast!" said Skirty Marm.

"But Skirt, we did it!" protested Old Noshie. "Give her the wretched Power Hat so we can go home!"

"Sorry, Badsleeves," said Skirty Marm. "I'm keeping it. If I let you have it, how do I know you won't turn into another Mrs A.? How do I know you'll keep your promise and free the cat-slaves?" Gently, she picked up the exhausted Mendax. "We've done our bit. Now it's up to you to rule this island with true EQUALITY and JUSTICE."

Badsleeves scowled and stamped her foot. The other S.L.A.W. witches, however, looked pleased.

"She's got a point," said Binbag. "You must admit, Badsleeves, you were getting rather big for your stockings. I don't think we should trust any of our leaders with that Hat. It doesn't seem to bring out the best in a witch."

Badsleeves sighed. "Oh, I suppose you're right. But what will you do with it, Skirty? How do I know you won't try to be queen?"

"Pish and posh!" Skirty Marm said scornfully. "I've got better things to do. We'll take this Power Hat back to our new country and make sure it never falls into the wrong hands again – not even Mrs A. will be able to call it back. I'm only going to use it for one small spell."

"What's that?" asked Old Noshie.

Skirty Marm grinned. "I'm collecting some Lost Property."

She closed her eyes, and up flashed the magic letters in her mind. *Options: 1. Snatch bloomers off Sneevil. 2. Snatch bloomers off Sneevil, and smack her. 3. Snatch bloomers, and change Sneevil into a little Yellow-Stocking.*

"Number three again," said Skirty Marm. "That'll teach her!"

8

A New Era

The first proper General Election on Witch Island was a magnificent event. Once the Purples and Greens realized Mrs Abercrombie no longer held the ultimate power, they were no longer terrified of her. This time, the Hat was not lost at sea, but firmly on the purple head of Skirty Marm. Noshie and Skirty were national heroines. They rode around on their broomsticks, shouting, "Vote Badsleeves!"

Mendax was having the time of his life. For once, he was allowed to make grand speeches to his heart's content. His finest moment had come when Old Noshie told him to free the kitchen cat-slaves. The poor creatures were afraid at first – but when they saw Mrs Abercrombie stomping out of the palace, they threw Mrs Wilkins in the sink and smashed all the crockery, and their happy purrs could be heard for miles.

Whether snooty or humble, the cats were now free citizens.

Skirty Marm kept the Power Hat on her head at all times so that it could not be tampered with. She had no idea what to do with it, but was determined to take it off the island. Several Purple-Stockings had offered her large sums of money if she would sell them the Hat. Mrs Abercrombie herself, now running her election campaign from a small and obscure cave, offered to share the Hat with Skirty. But Skirty Marm could not be bought.

"Think what you could do with it!" Badsleeves said rather wistfully. "Aren't you even tempted?"

"No," said Skirty Marm. "I've punished Sneevil, and that's my limit."

She was stern when Badsleeves suggested the Hat should be put in the Island Museum.

"Sooner or later, someone would smash the glass case and nick it," she said, looking hard at Badsleeves. "I'm going to think of a really safe place to hide it."

"We can ask Mr B.," said Old Noshie happily. Both witches were looking forward to telling their friend about their adventures. It was fun being national heroines, but Witch Island was no longer their real home. As Old Noshie put it, "Our hearts belong with the humans now."

They could not leave the island, however, until they had cast their votes at the election. Badsleeves won by a huge majority. As soon as she promised to lift the stocking freeze and put an end to the hated Broom Tax, she became hugely popular. Most Greens, and even Purples, were happy to vote for her. Though Mrs Abercrombie was still the cleverest individual witch, her power did not amount to much with thousands of Purples ranged against her.

"Let this day become a National Holiday," declared Chancellor Badsleeves, "in honour of the two brave witches who gave us LIBERTY!"

Old Noshie and Skirty Marm blushed with pride until their ears sizzled. They were invited to one hundred and sixty-four election night parties, and actually went to fifty-eight of them before Old Noshie fell asleep with her face in a bat tart.

"Dear me," said Mendax, "how very gratifying it is to be appreciated."

Chancellor Badsleeves had asked Mendax to be Minister of Cats in her new government. Old

Noshie and Skirty Marm were very surprised when they heard he had refused this honour.

"I thought you'd love it," said Skirty Marm. "You're such a show-off."

"Once, perhaps," purred Mendax. "But I would miss my dear vicar far too much. And I couldn't leave him to write his own sermons."

"I'm glad you're coming home with us," Old Noshie said. "Know what, Mendax? If you stayed here, I'd miss you!"

"Oddly enough," said Skirty Marm, "so would I."

Mendax smoothed his whiskers. "I once

hated witches, but you two have showed me that you're not all like Mrs Wilkins." (Mrs Wilkins was in prison for cruelty to cats; Mendax had been chief witness at her trial.)

The following morning, Old Noshie, Skirty Marm and Mendax prepared to fly home. A large crowd gathered to see them off, and the Green-Stocking Brass Band played their latest hit, "March of the Main Sewer".

Chancellor Badsleeves awarded each of the three friends the Order of the Prune (First Class). Mendax tied on his saucepan crash-helmet, and climbed into his basket. The Power Hat was making Skirty Marm's head ache but, taking no chances, she rammed it down firmly across her forehead. The brooms set their course for home, and the witches looked over their shoulders at Witch Island until it vanished into a black speck in the black ocean.

They arrived home at tea time, and Mr Snelling and Mr Babbercorn were overjoyed to see them. Mr Snelling was so happy, he put his back out trying to turn a cartwheel. Mendax immediately put on his flowery apron and rushed to the kitchen to bake a homecoming sponge.

The vicar and the curate were amazed at the sight of the Power Hat. It certainly looked very strange and sinister standing in the middle of the sitting room carpet, tall as Mr Babbercorn. The everlasting candle burned with a still, ghostly light.

"I don't like keeping a . . . a *thing* like this on church property," said Mr Babbercorn, shaking his head. "What on earth shall we do with it?"

"It has to be somewhere near humans, but where humans can't get it," protested Skirty Marm. "Didn't we tell you how the pants you lent protected us? Mrs A. could never call it back from here – not with all her magic!"

Mr Babbercorn frowned. "Would the new extension to the village hall count? I mean, that's church property – and they've just dug the foundations."

"Perfect!" cried the witches.

As soon as it was quite dark, the curate and the witches carried the Power Hat through the streets of the village, and buried it deep in the foundations of the hall extension.

"It'll be covered in thirty metres of concrete tomorrow," said Mr Babbercorn breathlessly, tucking his spade under one arm.

"Good riddance!" said Skirty Marm. "I was getting so sick of wearing it. You can't even have a simple little thought in case it turns magic."

"Uneasy lies the head that wears the crown," Mr Babbercorn said solemnly.

They turned their backs on the Power Hat, and went back to the vicarage to eat Mendax's cake. The little cat made Mr Snelling very proud when he described his thrilling adventures without telling a single lie. Finally, yawning noisily, Old Noshie and Skirty Marm climbed the one hundred and eighty-six steps to their belfry.

It was bliss to lay their tired heads down on their Christmas cushions. The moonlight fell softly upon the great church bells. The woods and fields around them were cloaked in a velvet silence. All was peace.

Tired as they were, however, the witches could not fall asleep at once. The Power Hat had been buried, and would glow in secret under the village hall until the crack of doom. They could never forget it.

"Are you awake, Skirt?" asked Old Noshie.

"Yes," said Skirty Marm.

"I've been thinking," said Old Noshie, "that I've really had enough of magic."

"Me too," said Skirty Marm. "But I can't help wondering – has magic had enough of us?"

Kate Saunders
BELFRY WITCHES 3
Red Stocking Rescue

Old Noshie and Skirty Marm are terribly upset. Although they've
promised to be good, Mr Babbercorn won't let them be
bridesmaids at his wedding. And Mendax the cat isn't even
allowed to sing a solo!

But then deep, dark magic turns Alice, Mr Babbercorn's bride-to-
be, into a snail. Who is the culprit – and can two brave witches
(and one clever cat) cook up a spell that will save the wedding
from disaster?

Kate Saunders
BELFRY WITCHES 4
Power Hat Panic

Tranters End is full of excitement. A rich and mysterious old lady
has moved into a ruined cottage in the woods, and now she's
buying everyone presents!

But Old Noshie and Skirty Marm aren't fooled. This creepy
creature may look like a sweet old granny, but she's none other
than their worst enemy – monstrous Mrs Abercrombie, Queen of
the Witches. And she's come to reclaim her Power Hat . . .